GRIND

**Adapted by Robin Wasserman
from the screenplay by Ralph Sall**

SCHOLASTIC INC.

New York   Toronto   London   Auckland   Sydney   Mexico City
New Delhi   Hong Kong   Buenos Aires

No part of this publication may be reproduced in whole or in part, or stored in a retrieval system, or transmitted in any form or by any means, electronic, mechanical, photocopying, recording, or otherwise, without written permission of the publisher. For information regarding permission, write to Scholastic Inc., Attention: Permissions Department, 557 Broadway, New York, NY 10012.

ISBN 0-439-62188-7

Copyright © Gaylord Films LLC.

Published by Scholastic Inc. All rights reserved.

SCHOLASTIC and associated logos are trademarks and/or registered trademarks of Scholastic Inc.

Designed by Keirsten Geise

12 11 10 9 8 7 6 5 4 3 2 1   3 4 5 6 7 8 9/10

Printed in the U.S.A.

First printing, October 2003

Eric
Eric Rivers — "Sponsor Me" Video, take 1

Hi. Hey, what's up. Ahh — I'm Eric Rivers and I would really love to be sponsored. My skating is solid, and I'm really committed to going out there and taking it to the next level. I could really use a new deck. Mine's pretty thrashed. And I think I've really honed my style since my last tape.

Anyway, I hope you can see something even though Matt keeps screwing with the camera.

Check out my latest trick. You're gonna want your name all over it. The 360 flip over the hip. So call me. Anytime, day or night . . . Daytime you might need to leave a message 'cause right now I'm tryin' to clock some dollars slingin' the fast food un- til the skating comes through. Thanks. Peace out, take it easy, and all that.

Was that okay? I think it was pretty hot. We'll cut out the part where I beefed it. . . .

Morning.

Not again.

I slammed off the alarm and dragged myself up out of bed. Won- dered: When I'm a righteous skater on the pro circuit heading out to meet my fans, will mornings be any easier?

Doubtful.

I threw on a T-shirt and some shorts and stumbled toward the mirror. (Hey, a guy's got to have a certain style if he's gonna make it to the pros, right?) Did a quick inventory: rumpled clothes, groggy eyes, wild hair . . . total perfection.

Of course . . . the world can always wait for perfection. And my bed — or what I could see of it, buried beneath a pile of dirty clothes and skater zines — looked tempting.

I almost bagged the morning and dove back under the covers, but then I spotted it. The banner taped to the top of my mirror. I made it myself, and it gets me every time:

WORK AND PLAY ARE THE SAME THING UNDER DIFFERENT CIRCUMSTANCES.

Sad but true. And that meant it was time to go to work.

I tossed my "sponsor me" tape into my backpack, grabbed my board, and — with one last look at that nice, soft bed — headed out the door.

∞∞∞∞∞

It was worth it.

As soon as I hit the street, I was in the groove — I hit a flip trick solid, first try, and then railed down the steps and flipped off the banister. And that was just the warm-up.

That's right, skateboarding. It was my work, my play, my life. And if you're thinking that sounds like a waste of time, well, you've probably never skidded down the street with the wind in your hair, feeling like there's nothing in the universe but you, your deck, and the ground rushing between your feet. You've probably never defied gravity, flown through the air, and landed a perfect 360. You've probably never boarded — and in that case, let's face it, you've never really lived.

Every morning, every afternoon, I grabbed my board and hit the street — the neighborhood was my own private skate course. I scaled banisters, veered off benches, jumped Dumpsters, and totally freaked out any sorry suburban joggers who got in my way. Every day, no questions asked, because I was in training — I was making it to the pros, and nothing was going to stand in my way.

Except — I screeched to a stop, feeling like I was forgetting something. Wasn't there something else I was supposed to do today?

Oh yeah.

Graduate.

Dustin
Dustin Knight — "Sponsor Me" Video, take 1

My name is Dustin Knight and I'd really like to be on your team. But I need to know if it's going to work out because I'm supposed to be going to college in the fall and my parents want to make sure that I'm able to make a decent living and stand on my own two feet. Right now I'm grindin' all summer working for peanuts. So let me know if I can do better with you, 'cause maybe I can defer my studies for a while. . . . Plus, I always keep my wheels clean.

I couldn't believe I was going to be late for my own high school graduation. My parents were going to *kill* me.

Not that it sounded like I was missing much. I certainly wasn't missing the oh-so-fascinating graduation speech they were piping through the empty hallways. Here's a perfect example of what's wrong with the people who run high schools. They just don't think. I mean, you have to imagine that anyone who was still in the hallway during the graduation would be there because they *wanted* to miss the speeches — so why pipe them in? Just one last chance to torture us, I guess. And it was torture:

". . . so just as this is the end of the road for us as a unit, it's a new beginning for all of you. Some of you are entering college in the fall, pursuing the endlessly outstanding opportunities of the corporate world, while others are saying hello to the lower earning potential of the working world. A world of adults and adult responsibilities. No more 'excused absences' and no more makeup tests. You'll have your ups and downs. But just remember, whether you fail or succeed, it's the journey that counts. . . ."

This is the new beginning I'm supposed to be looking forward to? A world of adult responsibilities and low earning potential?

Speaking of low earning potential, where was Eric? If I was late, he was —

Oh, of course. Speeding by me on his board, knocking my cap onto the ground. Totally typical.

The speaker was still going: ". . . and so, as we look ahead, whether promising or hopeless, the future is OURS!!"

Eric looked about as excited by our bright future as I was. But still, graduation is graduation, right?

"We're heinously late," I said, pulling him down the hall.

Eric shrugged. "They don't have anything over us anymore. We're done!"

∽∽∽∽∽

Graduation was . . . well, graduation. You know the drill: caps, gowns, speeches, marching, blah, blah, blah. But there was one good thing — one really good thing: Like Eric said, we were finally done.

After the ceremony, we pulled off our caps and gowns and left school one last time.

"I've got to get this home before it gets wrinkled," I said, holding up my diploma.

"I can't believe I even got one of these," Eric said, looking at his diploma like it had just crawled out of a sewer. He shook his head and tossed it in a garbage can. I couldn't believe it.

"Hey! You're going to need this!" I yelled, fishing it out of the garbage.

"What for?"

"For whatever it is you're gonna do."

"What do you mean whatever *I'm* gonna do? *We* are turning pro."

Oh god, not again.

"Come on," I said, disgusted. "That's never really gonna happen."

Eric just grinned. "We're getting sponsored, remember?"

Maybe I could knock some sense into him this time. "Come on, Eric. Every kid who can rail thinks they're goin' pro. You need something to fall back on. That's why I'm going to college." We must have had this conversation a hundred times, but nothing I said ever seemed to sink in. I don't think he believed I was actually going through with the whole college thing.

"No way. I won't let you throw your life away on something stupid like that." Eric's eyes were blazing. "We're gonna make it together. You're comin' with me."

"I can't."

"You can."

"I can't."

"You *can*."

I hate it when he does this to me. I mean, the kid is my best friend, but once he gets something into his head, it's like he just ignores any inconvenient facts that don't fit into his plans. And this time he was really living in a fantasy world.

"Look," I finally said, "I can't do it. I'm just facing reality, Eric. I mean, you think you're turnin' pro with you skatin' on that deck? It's totally thrashed!"

Pay dirt! No way he could deny that one — Eric looked down at his deck, which is definitely, absolutely thrashed. But . . . never underestimate the power of the deluded.

"This isn't about my deck, Dustin," he said. "It's about living your dreams."

"So stop dreaming. It's time to wake up."

Eric couldn't stop smiling, and I knew that in his head, he was seeing us all out there on the pro circuit together, sponsored superstars. And I knew then that nothing I said could stop him. "It's all or nothing, dude," he said.

Eric

CRA-A-A-CK.

That was it. The sound that no boarder — at least, no boarder with run-down equipment and a minimum-wage job — ever wants to hear. My board was beyond thrashed. Oh well, at least I was in the right place at the right time. I picked up the pieces and headed into the skate shop.

Bad luck — Greg was working the counter. Not exactly the person most likely to get sweet-talked into giving me a new board for free. But hey, life is about taking chances, right? Besides, he was zoned out in front of the TV, watching some totally insane skateboard slams. Maybe he'd be so blissed out by the video that he'd just toss a new deck at me. Worth a try . . .

"Hey, Greg, how's it going?"

"Not as good as it was before you walked through my door."

O-kay. Time for some fast talking.

"Wanna check out my new 'sponsor me' tape?"

"Is it any different than your last three?" he asked.

Ouch. That was cold. But I was a man on a mission. I smiled, trying to ooze some confidence. "Totally. I almost nailed the three-sixty flip over the hip."

"You land that and *I'll* sponsor you." Greg paused, looking me up and down. "You gonna buy something this time?"

Low blow. "C'mon, I'm one of your biggest customers," I reminded him. "I'm always here!"

"Yeah, but you never spend any money."

Speaking of that . . . No time like the present. I put my broken board down on the counter. "It'd be so cool if you could flow me a new board," I said, trying to strike the right balance between casual and desperate. "Mine's all finished."

That's when it happened. Before Greg could answer, the door opened, and in walked *Bam*. You know who he is — everyone knows who Bam is. Totally awesome skater, big star on the pro tour, and, apparently, loyal customer of *my* skate shop.

He rolled up to the counter. "Yo, hook me up with one of my decks."

Greg didn't cop any attitude with this guy. "No prob, Bam," he said.

I still couldn't get over it. "That's Bam. Here. In person." And then Bam actually turned toward me!

"You're comin' down to the demo, right?" he asked. "Check it out."

Are you kidding me? "Wouldn't miss it."

Greg pulled down a deck and tossed it to Bam, who fumbled it, and the deck crashed to the floor. I was down there like lightning and picked it up for him. I wiped it off and handed it back to him — Bam didn't deserve a dirty deck.

"Righteous," he said.

Righteous? I was righteous? Dude, this was my chance. "Hey, Bam! How's it going, man?" Bam kind of smiled and started backing away, but I just kept talking. "I saw you at the Springfield contest last year. You rule, man!"

"Cool . . ." He was already halfway out the door. I opened my mouth to say something else, but before I could, he muttered, "Look, I gotta go. Later."

And just like that, he was gone.

If you can believe it, Greg was actually smiling. "He was one of my regulars before he got sponsored," he said. "Just like you, except he actually bought stuff."

Suddenly, I got a brilliant idea. . . .

"Here's the deal," I said. "You flow me a new board . . ."

"For free . . ." Dude, was Greg actually on my wavelength?

"Exactly," I said, getting excited. "You hook me up with a new board. I skate like a stud on it and I tell everyone where I got it." I took a deep breath. "*You* can sponsor me."

Greg didn't even pause. He just turned to his wall of boards, pointed, and asked, "Which one do you want?"

Was this actually happening? "Hook me up with a Shorty's like Bam's. That'd be so righteous."

Greg smiled. Again. (Twice in one day — it had to be a world record for the guy.) "No problem." He held the board out toward me, and then — "For you, I can do about one-forty. Plus tax."

Busted. No way did I have that kind of cash. Well . . . desperate times call for desperate measures. I pointed behind him. "Um, how much is that right there?"

Greg looked confused. "What? The duct tape?"

"You got different colors?"

"It's duct tape."

Sometimes, you gotta do what you gotta do.

Dustin

The day after graduation. The first day of the rest of my life. And what was I doing? Same thing I did yesterday, same thing I'd do tomorrow. Skating to Eric's house and listening to my best friend talk up his nonexistent future as a pro. One small difference today — his thrashed board was, if possible, even more totally thrashed. It looked like it might be held together by duct tape . . . but I didn't have the heart to ask. And, of course, it didn't seem to stop him.

"Don't you ever feel like there's something more for you out there?" he asked. "Something great? Something bigger?"

"I guess."

"That's what I'm sayin'." Here it comes. "As soon as we get sponsored, we'll be livin' the life. . . ."

"But we're not sponsored," I reminded him. "We skate for fun." We headed into his backyard.

"Come on," Eric said. "We're totally good enough to go pro and you know it."

"I did the math, Eric. It's hopeless. There's something like fifty-three guys on the planet who make a living skating, and there's about a million wanna-bes like us." I mean, don't get me wrong — I want to be a pro skater as much as the next guy, but can I help it if I'm a realist? It was time to take a stand. "I'll send my tape in, but until a sponsor backs a tour bus up to my front door, I'm gonna sling fast food all summer to pay for fall semester. Period."

"I can't believe you're bailing on me!"

I'd had enough. "Give it up already. Matt listened to you and look where it's got him! Nowhere! He's a total stain!"

"Matt knows which end is up," Eric said.

At that moment — "Aaaaaaah!"

And that would be Matt.

Our supposedly savvy friend, who'd chosen this instant to skate off Eric's roof. In his underwear. He sailed through the air — skateboard, underwear, and all — and splashed down toward the pool.

Yeah, Matt knew which end was up. He just didn't care.

Matt
Matt Jensen — "Sponsor Me" Video, take 7

Hi, everybody out there in professional skating land. . . . My name is Matt Jensen and . . .

> *Lemme start over. That was lame.*
>
> *You'll cut this part out, right? 'Cause I really want to show my primo stuff.*
>
> *Okay, I'm starting over.*
>
> *Matt Jensen's the name. As you can see, right now I've got this stupid cast on my limb from trying a gnarly trick combination of my own creation. So I thought I'd describe to you the tricks I'd land if you sponsored me. . . . Okay, here goes. I'll do a half cab noseslide. A tailslide switch crooked grind. Oh, look, I just nollied an awesome triple set!*

Dude! That was totally righteous!

Wet. But totally righteous! I grabbed my board and paddled over to the side of the pool. Dustin and Eric were looking down at me, totally impressed by my smooth moves. Hey, brainstorm — maybe I should include *this* on my sponsorship video. Blow those pros away. Yeah, and I could add a 360 on the way down and grind the pool floor before coming up for air and — What? I looked up at Eric, who seemed pissed. Did he say something?

"Dustin's bailing on us," he said.

You're bustin' up my brainstorm for that news flash? "What's new? Dustin always bails."

"I'm not bailing, you idiot," Dustin said. I love it when he gets all red and starts looking like his head's going to pop off. "I'm always gonna skate."

Eric wasn't buying it. "Yeah, you say that, but other stuff comes up —"

"It's called higher education."

I wanted to say, Dude, look at me — primo example of why higher education is a waste of time. When I graduated, did I flush my life down that big college toilet? No way — I'm out here living it up in the University of the Real World. This is life, man. This is the stuff!

But that seemed like a lot of effort.

Besides, Eric was on a roll.

"Before you know it," he said, "you're a middle-aged bald guy with a gut. Then your wife leaves you and you're left wondering what happened to the days when all that mattered was the feel of the wood under your feet."

And speaking of middle-aged burnouts, out walked Eric's dad. Man, Mr. Rivers is a total pill. Look at the way the guy dresses — monogrammed bathrobe? Matching slippers? And catch the attitude:

"Get that moron out of the pool!" (Guess who the moron is. It's such a trip to tee that guy off.) "I should've burned that skateboard the day you brought it home . . . and when is Matt gonna relinquish his death grip on our premises? Have you smelled it around here lately? It's like an open sewer!"

Dude, rude much? I'm floating right here — like, I can totally hear you.

Eric's cool with it, though. "Good to see you, too, Dad."

"We need to talk!" Now the guy's face was getting all red, just like Dustin's.

"Can't right now. We're late. . . ."

And then we all stopped and stared. Because *Christy* had just strutted out of the house. That's Mr. Rivers' girlfriend. And she is a *total* Betty. I mean, we're talking hot. I just don't know what she's doing with the old man.

"Hi, sugar pop." Mr. Rivers waved to his hottie.

I batted my eyes. "I wish he'd stop calling me that."

Mr. Rivers shot me a dirty look, then turned back toward Christy. He pulled her in for a big fat kiss. If you've got it, flaunt it, I guess — and dude, he's got it. Eric just looked grossed out. But how would you feel if your dad was dating a dream girl and you were only dating, well, in your dreams?

Mr. Rivers ripped himself away from Christy's luscious lips long enough to finish his lame lecture. "Remember our deal . . ."

"Dad —"

" 'Dad' nothing. We had a deal. Either you're in school or you're working with me at the hardware store." He and Christy walked off.

I pulled myself out of the pool and was going to throw on my clothes but, okay, so they're kinda rank. Besides, Dustin was standing by the side of the pool looking so clueless, with his back to me, and, when opportunity knocks . . .

"Aaaaah!" Bull's-eye! Dustin went flying into the pool, and I jumped on top of him. Total chaos. Splashing. Wrestling. Screaming. (Who knew Dustin screamed like a girl?) Totally righteous.

Eric grabbed his board and walked off. "I'm gonna go skate."

Whatever, dude. His loss.

Dustin

"What seems to be the problem?" I plastered a smile on my face — and tried to hold my breath so that I wouldn't have to smell the raggedy, scraggedy-looking guy waving a receipt in my face.

"Yeah, I ordered the tummy killer ranchero and I got the double chunk gut bomb with cheese by mistake." I leaned back — spit was flying out of this guy with every word. "I'd like what I ordered."

"But you already ate the gut bomb," I said. Reminding myself, *The customer is always right. The customer is always right. Even when he's a rank loser. The customer is always right.*

"I can't help it if I didn't figure it out until I swallowed it," scraggle-tooth said.

I couldn't stop myself. "Do you really think you need another?"

Big mistake. My manager shot over to us. It's like he's got some sort of radar for customer service infractions. He stepped in front of me and put on his big, greasy Chili 'N' Such smile. "Our policy clearly states every customer will be served his order to his satisfaction. A replacement will be given as long as the customer can produce his receipt. . . ."

Ugh. I inched away. I'd heard this one before. Too many times. Welcome to my life. My lame, lame life as a proud Chili 'N' Such employee, where I have the great honor of slinging inedible food onto the trays of fat slobs who wouldn't know the difference between a bowl of "chili" and a bowl of . . . well, you can imagine. You can also imagine what a joy it was to work for Cameron, a stuck-up greaseball who thinks managing Chili 'N' Such is his life's calling.

And then Eric darted in — late. Don't get me wrong, I'm no model employee, but Eric is like a magnet for Cameron trouble. And he usually drags me down with him.

"You're, you're late, Rivers," Cameron mumbled, still helping the smelly dude give himself a slow heart attack. "Consider this an official warning."

Eric got to work on the chili prep assembly line, ladling huge globs of chili into the bowls. I knew the drill. Chili. Two scoops cheddar. One scoop onion. Next bowl. Chili . . .

Only Eric wasn't paying attention to what he was doing. Unfortunately for him, Cameron was. I sat back to watch the show.

"All kitchen workers must have their hair net on at all times," Cameron told him.

Eric slipped on the hair net. What a joke. If he looked that bad in it, I couldn't even imagine how I must have looked.

"And it's two scoops cheddar," Cameron said. "One scoop onion."

"Right," Eric said.

Cameron smiled and put his arm around Eric. I could see where this was going. Cameron liked to think of himself as a role model for us aspiring fast-food managers.

"You know, Eric, you've got potential," he said, pulling Eric tighter toward him. "If you'd just apply yourself, there's no telling how high you'll fly in the Chili 'N' Such family. So go get 'em, deputy." Cameron walked off, thinking, I'm sure, that he had just given Eric a new reason to live.

Little did he know, Eric was still stuck on the old one. "Only two more hours until the demo," he reminded me. "We gotta jet outta here early so we can get up close."

"No way. I need the overtime."

"You gotta loosen up," he said, getting frustrated.

But as far as I was concerned, I'd been loose long enough. "Sixty-eight more days and I've got my freshman year covered." I tried not to think of sixty-eight more days at Chili 'N' Such. What a nightmare. And then Cameron came back, and the nightmare was complete. He shoved a mop in my face.

"Get in gear, Knight. The men's room hasn't been cleaned for days — why don't you show a little team spirit and see if you can make it sparkle in there?"

Oh, gross. Eric looked at me like, See what you're in for?

"What?" I muttered. "I need this gig. But in September, I'll be in college and you'll still be here."

Cameron wasn't done with us yet. He turned to Eric. "And you, there's a birthday at table thirteen."

"Oh god." Eric knew what that meant.

"I need you in the bean suit." Cameron grinned an evil grin.

"No, please, not the bean suit!"

ംംംംം

Check it out: Eric Rivers, skateboard stud . . . pro-in-training . . . giant bean.

"It's your birthday. Hooray. It's your birthday, okay!" He was surrounded by employees playing kazoos — you could tell they were just thankful they weren't the ones in costume. "So eat chili and such, there's no such thing as too much, and happy happy happy birthday to youuuuu."

Ohhh, I felt for the guy. Even pulling bathroom duty was better than the bean suit. Although . . . I looked down at my disgusting mop, my dirty shoes, and took a big whiff of my newly nasty self.

Okay, maybe not.

Eric

Thank god I finally got out of that place. A full day at Chili 'N' Such would be enough to drive anyone out of their mind. But all my troubles faded away as soon as I hit the big pro skate demo. Matt, Dustin, and I edged our way to the front of the crowd, and it was worth it. Jimmy Wilson's team put on a radical show and the crowd went crazy.

"These guys can skate," I said, wishing I were out there with them. "Check out Jimmy Wilson."

Even Dustin was with me on that one. "Insane," he yelled over the noise of the crowd. "He really put a dream team together this year!"

When Jimmy finished skating, he launched himself into the crowd. I had to give the guy credit, he was nice enough to the kids, smacking their hands, signing autographs. But it didn't take him long to move on to his real reward: the girls.

"Look at those girls lining up to get a crack at him," Dustin said. I could hear the envy in his voice. "And I'm talking real talent."

He was right, the girls were totally hot, and it was clear that all they wanted was Jimmy, Jimmy, Jimmy. And that was just the beginning. "It's more than that," I said. "You get to skate for a living. He's like a rock star!"

"I wonder if they have to do their own laundry," Matt mused.

He had a lot to learn about fame. "Pros don't need to do laundry," I told him. "When they're finished wearing something, like a shirt, they just throw it out and pick up a fresh one. It's all free."

Matt grinned. "I want that."

"Dude, you *need* that," Dustin said. "I think you need to burn your rank gear."

Seriously, do us all a favor. "Man, if you took that shirt off, I think it might be able to make its way through the crowd on its own," I said, only half joking.

Matt turned on both of us. "What're you trying to say?"

I just shook my head and looked at Dustin. "You reek," he said. "Like an armpit. Dipped in garlic."

My turn. "Soap and water. Look into it."

But nothing fazes Matt. I don't think he cared that you could practically see the stink waves rising off of him. So I guess we were stuck with him — you take the good with the bad, right?

We pushed our way through the crowd, and suddenly I spotted Jimmy Wilson's tour bus. It was unbelievable. I pointed it out to the guys. "Can you imagine riding in that?"

"Yeah." Matt got a dreamy look in his eyes. "The free stuff, the girls, the royalty checks, the autograph signings . . . Did I mention the girls?"

But I barely heard him. I was too busy looking at Her. Gazing at her, actually. She was the most beautiful babe I had ever seen. I couldn't take my eyes off her — it was like there was no one else in the world but the two of us. She was pure perfection — golden hair, luscious lips, soulful eyes, and that body . . . man, she was amazing.

And suddenly, she was looking right at me.

I opened my mouth, but no words came out. I wanted her too much — and she was about to slip away. And then —

"Hi." The goddess spoke!

"Hey," I called out. My mind was racing. What next? Should I wave? Should I call out again? What could I say that would make her come closer — that would make her come toward me and never leave?

And just as I had gathered up my courage to say something, anything, my so-called friend Matt lifted up his arm to smell his nasty cast. Lifted it right in front of me, blocking the girl — the woman — from view. And when I pushed his arm out of the way, it was too late.

Just like that, she was gone.

Matt

Ahhhh . . .

So many lovely ladies, so little time.

Does life get any better? Surrounded by my two best friends and a lot full of ladies. There go some right now. "Check out the honeys," I said, pointing the babes out to my bros. "Can't get enough of them." Eric just looked at me like I had a booger hanging out of my nose. Oh. Maybe I did. Whatever. No time to waste. I planted myself in front of the closest hottie.

"Hey, wassup?"

"Hey." She didn't smile. Okay, she didn't even look at me. But maybe that was just her thing.

"Wassup? I mean, I already said that."

"Can you please move, in case one of the skaters looks over here?"

Uh, excuse me? "I'm a skater."

Now she was looking at me. "Oh yeah?"

"Really. I'm not skating today 'cause I'm thrashed." I showed her my cast. She could've cared less. Okay, that's it. No one blows off the

Matt-man and gets away with it. I shoved my arm in her face. "Here, smell my cast. Whiff it!"

She pulled away. My sweat stench gets 'em every time. "Does it smell more like pee or pepperoni?"

And, of course, the hottie ran away. So much for that.

Eric and Dustin were staring at me.

"And you wonder why you can't get a date?" Eric said. Pretty harsh, especially coming from the dateless wonder.

"Hey, I'm in a dry spell," I complained.

Then Dustin chimed in. "To be in a dry spell, you have to have had a 'wet' spell."

Point taken. There was nothing I could say to that.

Matt's rule: When you don't have a comeback . . . change the subject. I pointed behind them. "Product toss!" And before they could say anything, I ran over to the product toss, pushing some shorties out of my way. Little kids don't need product like *I* need product.

Mission accomplished. I headed back to Eric with a new board for him in tow. "Had to rip it out of the hands of a ten-year-old," I said triumphantly, handing it over.

Dude, who wouldn't want me?

Eric

So I was up one board, down one goddess. It looked like I'd be breaking even for the day.

Unless.

Unless we could talk our way in to see Jimmy Wilson and finally kick our sponsor search into high gear. I pulled the guys over to the tour bus. I just had a feeling that this was going to be our day.

But before we could get in, we had to get past the hulking security guy who was guarding the bus. He was looking off into the distance, and the last thing I wanted to do was get this guy's attention, but . . .

"We're here to see Jimmy," I said, in my best smooth-talking tone. The security guy turned to face me, and that's when I saw it —

"Oh my freakin' lord!" Rude, I know. But I couldn't help myself — half the guy's face was covered in the ugliest, gnarliest scab I had ever seen! He looked around to see what I was getting so excited about — and a giant drop of yellow pus dripped off his face and splattered on my shoe. Could life get any grosser?

I said the first thing that popped into my head. "Dude, I am not looking at your face!" Smooth, Eric. Real smooth.

That pretty much did it — he was done with us. "No Jimmy, dude," he growled. "Not gonna happen. He's done for the day."

That's when we decided that maybe scabface wasn't our best bet for an intro. We spotted Jimmy's tour manager loading equipment into a luggage locker on the side of the bus. Maybe he'd be more helpful. Or at least, less disgusting.

I walked up to him. "We're skaters, man. We're looking for a sponsor and we just need Jimmy to check out our tapes. Just for a minute."

The guy looked me up and down. "Sure you do." He moved to a different locker and lifted the door — a mountain of videotapes poured out. Uh-oh. "That's just today's haul," he said.

I couldn't believe it. "You got all of these tapes from today?"

He smiled. " 'Sponsor me.' Two very popular words."

"How does Jimmy have time to watch all of those?" Dustin asked.

The tour manager looked at us like we were idiots. "He doesn't."

Okay, time for Plan B. I winked at the guy, lowered my voice. "Isn't there some way you could get us in to see Jimmy?"

"No." The manager turned to get on the bus. So much for Plan B. "But get yourselves out there. Work on your skating. Jimmy says you never know where you'll find the great skaters." And he closed the door behind him.

There was a moment of silence. No one wanted to be the first to say something.

Finally, Matt tried to smile. "I wouldn't call it being blown off, exactly. . . ."

"We got dissed and dismissed," Dustin said.

No way was I letting this be the end of things. I mean, dude, we had a destiny. I just needed to make the guys believe in it. "It's cool," I said. "We should be hearing back from some of the companies who've seen our tapes any day now."

Matt cleared his throat and looked down at the ground. "Thing is . . . I haven't actually gotten around to mailing out the videos yet."

"What?" I wanted to punch him.

"The lines at the post office are so long! It's a total day killer!"

Oh, I was going to kill him. That slacker! That loser! That —

Okay. Deep breath. Remember the power of positive thinking. And, once I thought about it, I came up with an idea. A totally awesome, brain-busting, brilliant idea. I beamed at the guys. "Actually, this is great!"

"It is?" Matt and Dustin were looking at me like I'd lost my mind.

"Yeah. It means we haven't been judged and rejected! It means that no one's seen us! It means we still have a chance!"

Dustin wasn't buyin'. "Does it include kicking Matt's lazy butt?"

"Hey, thanks to my 'lazy butt,' we can still visit that little town called hope!"

Dustin rolled his eyes and pushed Matt out of the way. Matt, of course, pushed back. But I didn't have time to get involved in that kind of thing anymore. I had a plan — and this time, it was going to work.

Dustin

Now, this was more like it. Chilling in Eric's basement, creaming Matt in Tony Hawk Pro Skater 4 (not too hard since Matt was half playing, half cutting off his cast with a handsaw) — I could have stayed there forever.

And then Eric came downstairs. That's when it all started.

"Start packing," he said, standing in the doorway. "We're going on tour."

"Great!" Matt threw down the saw. "When do we leave?"

I was a little more suspicious. "I don't believe it," I said. "Someone saw our tapes? Whose team are we on?"

Eric pulled something out of the bag he was holding. "Just check out these shirts," he said, holding one up for us. This fashion masterpiece featured a skating superhero with a bright cape — and printed underneath was SUPER DUPER SKATEBOARDS. You have got to be kidding me.

Eric looked so eager, so hopeful. "What do you think?"

I think you're insane, that's what I think. "I'm not wearing that," I told him. "The cape looks stupid. The whole thing sounds sketchy."

Even Matt was with me this time. "I've never heard of Super Duper Skates. . . ."

Eric looked a little embarrassed. "That's 'cause I just made it up."

I'd had enough of this. "You're losing it, Rivers."

"Hear me out. I made up this company so we'd have some credibility out on the road."

I jumped off the couch. "On the *road*?" I turned toward Matt. "I told you he was tweaked."

"No man, *listen*. We go out as a team, the three of us. You know we can skate as good as half these pros!"

I had a bad feeling about this — but still, I had to try. "Wake up and smell the desperation. . . ." But all we could smell in the room was Matt's newly cast-less arm. And if that's desperation, desperation *stinks*.

"Just hear me out," Eric said, refusing to give up. "Jimmy Wilson is the man, right? He *is* skateboarding. So we go out on the road, follow him." He was waving his arms wildly. "If we can get him to see us just once, he'll see we're the real deal! We'll totally get on that tour."

I glanced over at Matt, to see if he was as fed up as I was. Don't know what I was thinking, since Matt, as always, was in his own world. He poured a package of sea monkeys into a glass of water and then, if you can believe it, drank up. And I was counting on *him* to be a voice of reason?

It looked like this fight was all up to me.

"Sounds great," I said sarcastically. "But first, I've got to marry a supermodel and win the lottery."

"This is our last summer to make it happen for us," Eric said. "Now or never."

I was ready to vote for never, but Eric kept going. "We can either wait here forever and hope something happens with our lives, or we can do it ourselves!"

Then Matt came back down to this planet. "Where's the money for the trip coming from?"

Eric just looked at me.

No way. No freaking way could he be thinking what I think he's thinking. Not my money, not for this road trip to nowhere. "Now I really know you're tweaked."

"You can do it."

"I can't."

"You *can*."

"No way. Not a chance." Have I mentioned how much I hate it when he does this to me? And, big surprise, the two of them just kept going like I wasn't even in the room.

"What do we do for wheels?" Matt asked.

Eric grinned. Oh no — I sensed another big idea coming, and I was pretty sure I knew what it was. Eric wouldn't look at me — he knew I knew. "We need to find a van. . . ."

Just great. I knew what would come next. And I didn't like it one bit.

Matt

We needed Sweet Lou. And when you want to find Sweet Lou, there's only one place to look. The skate park.

You know Sweet Lou? Every town has one. You know, that kind of cool, kind of skeezy guy who does nothing all day but hang out in parking lots, trolling for chicks? That's Sweet Lou.

My idol.

And there he was, leaning against his van and chilling with two totally hot Betties. The dude has skills! The girls took off as we got near him, but I figured there'd be more where they came from.

"He's been cruisin' this park for Betties since we were freshmen," Dustin said, laughing. He and Eric never had the proper respect for Sweet Lou.

"Sweet Lou!" Eric called once we got close enough. "What's up?"

"Anything new with you losers?" Sweet Lou asked.

"Not much." Eric paused, and I could tell he was getting ready to strut his stuff. "Except we're turning pro. . . ."

"Yeah, I'll believe that when I see it."

"We're gonna get on the Jimmy Wilson tour," Eric said. "It's gonna be pretty cool. Only thing we need is a guy like you on the team."

You can say that again. Everyone needs a guy like Sweet Lou on the team. Let him do all the work reeling in the ladies, and my boys and I will pick up the leftovers. No pain, lots of gain.

"No doubt," Lou said. "But I've got all I need right here."

Dude doesn't know who he's dealin' with here. Eric doesn't take no for an answer. "C'mon, we're goin' cross-country. And you know what that means."

Sweet Lou smiled. "Yeah . . . no . . . What does it mean?"

"Betties from different area codes — unconquered territory!"

How could Sweet Lou turn down an offer like that? I was already drooling.

"It's tempting," he said. "But this is my spot, guys. My sweet spot."

Eric moved in for the kill. "But you graduated, like, six years ago! Isn't it time to move on?"

"I park it here year after year, wait for the girls to flow through. Lemme give you a taste of Sweet Lou's upcoming calendar. You caught those girls just now? That's just my Tuesday. You should see Friday."

Uhhh . . . what a life. . . .

Sweet Lou waved us away. "Sorry, boys. Have fun on your little road trip, but you can count me out."

And then we got the chance of a lifetime. A hot little number sauntered up to Sweet Lou, and we got to see the master at work. He gave her a slow, easy grin. "Hey, Wednesday . . ."

"It's Sandy." Dude, she so wanted him.

"Right . . ." The man was such a smooth talker.

"I've been trying you all day!" She looked up at him, batting her big Betty eyes.

"Sandy, chill. I told you — I'll call *you*. Don't get so extended!"

Man, he was totally working her. Sandy popped a piece of gum in her mouth and flicked her hair out of her eyes. "I'm fine with it and all," she said. "But my dad's crazed."

Sweet Lou almost fell over. "You told your dad?"

This didn't sound like it was part of the plan.

"Yeah. He says he's gonna kill you. Cut off your ears and dangle them from his rearview mirror."

Suddenly, a car screeched up, and this big guy jumped out — holding a baseball bat.

"Daddy!" Sandy shrieked. "Daddy" smashed his bat into Sweet Lou's taillight. It burst into a million pieces.

"Okay, get in," Sweet Lou said, trying to push past us.

"Really?" Eric asked.

"Now!" Sweet Lou piled us into the van and we took off, bat-man and Sandy running behind.

Eric patted Sweet Lou on the shoulder. "That *was* smooth," he said sarcastically. "How do you do it?"

Like I said, Eric's never had the proper respect for the master.

Eric

Everything was falling into place. Matt and Sweet Lou had piled a huge mound of stuff on my lawn, ready to be loaded into the van. After ducking inside, I was able to contribute an armload of junk food — we're growing boys, after all.

"Sweet," Matt said, impressed by the haul. "How'd you score all this food?"

"Fully raided my dad's kitchen. I took everything. We've got enough Slim Jims for a nuclear winter."

We started loading our stuff into the van. Laundry, food, CD's, blankets — everything you could ever need for a cross-country, follow-your-dreams, now-or-never road trip. Just as I tossed the last bag of chips into the back, Matt came up with a random female mannequin and an armful of spray cans.

He was grinning like a maniac. "One last thing before we're road ready." Ready, aim, fire!

A long time — and a *lot* of spray cans later — he had finished his masterpiece. And dude, it was definitely a work of art. Sweet Lou's van had been transformed into a radical, graffiti-covered touring machine. It was totally awesome.

Matt and I slapped hands and grabbed our packs — it was time to go.

But there was still something missing. . . .

Where was Dustin?

Dustin

Kidnapped! By my supposed best friends!

You wouldn't believe it if you'd seen it. They stormed into Chili 'N' Such and — literally — dragged me out to the van. I tried to stop them, tried to make them listen to reason, but did they listen? Oh no, not Eric, the man with a mission, and not Matt, his spastic minion.

"Wait!" I tried one last time. "I need my OT!"

"No, no you don't!" Eric opened the van's door and pushed me toward it.

"What about college?"

"You're not going!".

And just like that, I saw my future. And Eric was right — no college, no Chili 'N' Such, at least not this summer. This summer I was going on a ridiculous mission with my two best friends, and there wasn't anything I could do about it.

But if I had to go, I was at least going to be prepared. "Then I gotta go back to my place," I begged, "for my special pillow!"

We hopped in and the van screeched out of the parking lot — and, despite the ball of dread sitting at the pit of my stomach, I was still able to enjoy the look on Cameron's face when he came running out of the restaurant and saw his beloved summer staff take off into the sunset.

We left Cameron behind us, along with everything else — college funds, Chili 'N' Such, it was all part of my old life. Now we had nothing ahead of us but good tunes, good times, and the open road. Or, at least, that's what I tried to tell myself. This could be fun, right? It could be an adventure. . . .

Still, I made sure we swung by my house so we could pick up my lucky pillow. Something told me I was going to need it.

Eric

Day one. Kansas. The Pro-Am Contest, starring Jimmy Wilson. And featuring . . . the spectacular debut of Team Super Duper Skateboards!

The roar of the crowd echoed in the distance and, as we headed in from the lot, we passed by Jimmy Wilson's tour bus. It was totally a sign. Our first contest as pros — this was going to rock.

We headed for the check-in table, trying to ignore the punk-head losers who were taunting us from their tricked-out van. We weren't looking for any trouble, especially from stuck-up suburban skaters who played like they came from the 'hood. But they just wouldn't stop.

"Yo, yo, yo, I know you wanna-bes are not here to skate. . . ."

"Who's the wanna-be, fool?" Sweet Lou called over to them.

"Don't be talkin' like that," one of the guys said.

"I'm fi'in' ta buss' ya in your grill," another one called.

Then, of all people, *Dustin* opened his mouth. "It's your stank breath that's killin' me. Back off."

I pulled my guys away before they could say anything else — I didn't think we should start our first pro skate competition with black eyes and broken bones. Besides, I had just spotted something way more important than a bunch of gangster wanna-bes. Her.

The goddess from the skate demo — she was actually here!

Before I could say anything, she turned and started talking to one of the pro skaters. He obviously thought he was all that — I hoped that she could see right through him. But it didn't sound that way.

". . . yeah, the tour party's at the Rolling Deuce," she was saying. Ah, the sound of her voice . . . "Tonight at nine. Till whenever. It's gonna rage. All the pros are gonna be there — you should come by."

And then she turned away from him.

And toward me.

We locked eyes.

The rest of the world faded away.

She smiled. I smiled.

You could feel the energy crackling between us.

And then . . .

Matt stepped right in my way! I knocked him aside — but it was too late. She was gone. Again.

❧❧❧❧❧

I had to get this girl out of my mind. We were here to skate, not to mack on girls or (no matter how tempting it was) beat up on loser friends who kept getting in the way.

I led the guys up to the check-in table and warned them not to do

41

anything stupid. "Look, we're gonna let our skating do the talking." I turned toward the check-in guy, who was waiting to take my info. "Eric Rivers. Super Duper Skateboards. We're here to check in for the event."

The skate official checked his list.

Checked it again.

"Sorry, you're not registered."

"But we're sponsored skaters —" I started to say.

"Congratulations," he interrupted with a smirk. "That's great. Good for you. But you still have to be registered."

Why was this guy being such a pill? "Look, this is our first competition as a team. We drove all the way here." He didn't say anything, so I kept going. "I basically kidnapped Dustin. You *gotta* give us a chance."

The guy shook his head. "I'm sorry, but unless you preregistered for this event, you cannot participate."

And that was it. Our first pro skate event, over before it began. I didn't want to face the guys.

But I got them into this, and it was up to me to make it work. "Let's skate the lot," I suggested. "We'll wait Jimmy out."

It would work. It had to.

Matt

Dude, we were flyin' high. Hoisted a launch ramp onto the van and were skidding through some righteous tricks.

Eric tried to land his 360 over the hip again. Totally ditched out, again. But no matter, we were all in the zone.

So we weren't competing. So what? We were skating for the thrill of the skate, just us and the boards, the pavement, and the sky, and it was awesome.

I was railing through the lot, wind rushing through my hair, snot flying through the air, and I spotted those ghetto wanna-bes' van. Score! I tried to skate a gap and landed on the van's windshield.

CRA-A-ACK. That was the windshield.

THUD. That was me.

Uhhhhh.

I think I sprained my brain. And every bone in my body.

So much for the zone.

Dustin

"We can do this. Walk with confidence. Remember, we're pros. . . ."

I zoned Eric out. I was getting tired of these motivational speeches — he was starting to sound a little too much like Cameron. Besides, I was too nervous to pay attention to his stupid confidence-boosters. Here we were, sneaking into a pro party, hoping no one would notice that we were complete nonsponsored losers, and all I had to protect me from the hostile masses were Eric the dreamer, Sweet Lou the schemer, and . . .

"Dude, what did I just step in?"

And Matt, lord of the stench.

Matt kicked his foot up into Eric's face. "Smell that and tell me what I stepped in." Eric backed away like he was on wheels.

Matt scraped his foot on the pavement, but whatever *it* was, it wasn't coming off.

None of us ever know what to do about Matt, but Sweet Lou has his own . . . *unique* ideas. "Hold up a sec," he said, grabbing Matt. He lifted Matt's arms and sprayed breath spray under his pits, and then all over his body. Matt jumped back like he was being attacked, but Sweet Lou had him in a death grip.

"Ow, that stings!" Matt whiffed himself, looking confused. I hear that if you change an animal's smell, you'll drive it crazy because its distinct smell is its only way of identifying itself. Well, meet Matt.

And crazy was the word for it, because a step later, we passed a clown making balloon animals. Weird? Yes. Dangerous? I wouldn't think so, but Matt snapped — sidechecked the clown and knocked him onto the ground. Then just kept walking like nothing happened. Now, you tell me — crazy, or what?

"What's wrong with you?" I asked, afraid of the answer.

"I freaking hate clowns."

Eric

We were here. We were really here, at a pro party — and somewhere inside, my dream girl was waiting for me. The only thing standing between me and my destiny was an open door, a velvet rope, and — oh no. Another list.

A bored-looking woman stood in the doorway, holding her list and checking people off. I sidled up to her and tried my best to read a name off it upside down.

"Name?"

Reading upside down is harder than it looks. "I'm on the list. It's . . . Ka-Cha-Cha-ppell?"

She squinted at the list, then at me. "You mean, Sarah Chaplin?"

Um . . . Okay, just go with it. "Yeah — my mother wanted a girl."

"And I want you out of my face, liar." She moved on to the next person in line.

No way. No way was this day ending the way it began. I pulled the guys off to the side. We needed to come up with something. Fast.

"Any ideas?" I asked. All I got were blank stares. I had to step up, or we'd never get in.

"Just then, a bunch of total skating posers swaggered up to the door. They brushed us aside as if we were a bunch of nobodies. And of course, *their* names were on the list. But I had an idea. I gave the guys the high sign, and we all started imitating the posers. We slunk in behind them like we were part of their pretentious posse.

We were in!

∞∞∞∞∞

It was awesome. The room was filled with pro skaters — almost everyone I'd read about in the skater zines all these years was somewhere in the room. A hot DJ was spinning records, and the room was going crazy. But this was no time to get distracted. I sent Dustin and Matt on their way with a warning. "We're here to get on a team, so stay focused, spread out, and talk to as many pros as you can." I tried to look stern. "Now go mingle."

I spotted a pro I'd seen skate earlier that day — some blond groupie was hanging all over him, whispering in his ear. I just waited for him to notice me — I was sure he'd be glad to get rid of this ditz and talk some skating. Finally, he saw me.

"Can I help you?" he asked.

"I believe you can."

The pro looked at the girl, then at me. "How?"

"By hookin' me up with a sponsor."

"What?"

Was the dude a little slow? It wasn't that complicated a concept to grasp. "I wanna go on tour, hit the open road —"

"Dude, this is not a good time."

Too bad — this was the only time I had. "I understand but, see, I really think that I would totally bring some freshness to your whole deal." That sounded pretty cool, right? Would he go for it?

"Listen, bud. I'm a little busy here, so can we finish this fascinating conversation another time?"

Okay, that sounded better than nothing. "When?" I asked. "I can do it pretty much anytime."

The dude laughed. "No, you misunderstand me. I said 'another time,' but what I meant was 'go away.'"

Dustin

Eric was working the room like a pro, or like he thought he was a pro, trying to hook us up with a sponsor. I figured that since he was hard at work, well . . . maybe I should take some time to play. You can't be a good boy all the time, right?

I sat down next to a gorgeous girl, took a deep breath, and made the plunge. "What's your name?"

No answer.

"I think the music's too loud!" I shouted.

She looked bored. "I can hear you fine. I'm just not listening." And then she got up and walked away.

And this is supposed to be fun?

I spotted Matt putting the moves on another hot girl — the room was filled with them, and none of them seemed to have any interest in us. But this girl was different — she actually came up to Matt! Must have been the breath spray.

"Are you a skater?" she asked, smiling up at him. "I drove up from Springfield to meet a pro skater."

"Wow," Matt said. "So did I!"

"You're from Springfield?"

"No, I mean I came to meet some skaters."

The girl snorted and walked away, muttering, "Why do I always get stuck talking to the losers?"

Matt came over to join me. Misery loves company, I guess. So there we were, two losers. We stood against the wall, watching Sweet Lou lurk up behind the girl who blew me off. She was sitting down again — and she still looked *good*.

Sweet Lou sat next to her and shouted, "Hey, you want me?"

Suddenly, it all seemed worthwhile — to finally see Sweet Lou shot down like the rest of us. No way would a Betty like that go for a burnout like him. Not when she had her pick of the room. She took one look, wrinkled her nose, and shouted back, "Sure!"

Sweet Lou grabbed her hand and led her out of the room.

Are you kidding me? How does he do it?!

Eric

I was still stinging from that jerk blowing me off. But then I saw something that made it all just fade away. The goddess girl. She was back. Out on the floor, dancing like she didn't have a care in the world. Her blond hair swinging in her face, her arms waving through the air — it was the most beautiful, most graceful thing I'd ever seen.

Then suddenly, I almost choked. Bam came out of nowhere and started dancing next to her.

I didn't stand a chance.

Until . . . he left to get drinks.

I shook my head. If you can't beat 'em . . .

Join 'em. I pushed through the crowd toward the girl of my dreams. Just then, Matt and Dustin snagged me and launched into one of those break dances we perfected back in junior high. It was total old school and it was awesome. And just when I'd finally gotten the girl out of my mind and was totally consumed by the music, her face broke through the crowd — *she* was dancing with *me*.

"Hey!" she shouted, trying to make herself heard over the music.

"Hey!" We smiled at each other. So far, so good. Now if I could just take things to the next level, finally —

And that's when the security guards grabbed me and pulled me out of the party. Typical. The posers must've tipped them off. Man, those guys really had it in for us! I tried to catch the goddess's eye as they dragged me away, but she was already dancing with someone else. Probably a real pro, someone who actually belonged there. I don't know what she'd want with me anyway.

Not that it mattered. I didn't even know her name. I'd probably never see her again.

The security guys kicked us to the curb. And, to make the night complete, Sweet Lou managed to stay inside with the hotties. We were stuck on the curb, waiting for him to come out. Perfect. Just perfect.

"I think we made some real progress tonight," I said sarcastically. I was done being the team cheerleader.

At that moment, the posers drove by in a stretch Humvee limo. One of them stuck his head out of the window and threw a milkshake at the van. Then they sped off, laughing.

This trip was turning into a total nightmare.

Dustin

This trip was turning into a total nightmare.

Getting negged from the competition was bad enough.

Getting booted from the party was worse.

But this? This was the last straw.

"We're staying in this pit?" I asked in disbelief as we pulled up to the hands-down winner of the World's Skankiest Motel competition.

"Only the best for the Super Duper Skate Team," Eric said with a sigh. At least he'd stopped trying to make the best of absolutely everything.

We got out of the van and stopped at the edge of the nastiest pool I've ever seen. No *way* was I sleeping here — if the pool was this gnarly, imagine how disgusting the rooms might be. The four of us stood at the edge of this so-called pool, which was empty, except for the pile of pool furniture in its center and the mold growing all over the edges. There was a toilet perched at the very top of the pile. Classy.

Sleeping in the van last night stunk — but anything would be better than this. Or so I thought.

"And you said this wouldn't be fun," Eric said, trying to joke us out of our horror.

"I'm catching diseases just looking at it," I said with a shiver.

We backed away from the pool, around to the side of the motel — and right into a bell clerk who looked even freakier and nastier than the pool. I guess this motel didn't have a lobby. (And why would they need one? I was sure they'd never had a single guest before we were dumb enough to show up.) The guy was laid out on a deck chair, watching a TV that was plugged into an extension cord with about a million other plugs in it. A disaster waiting to happen, all around. But from the look of things, a fire would actually do this place some good.

He tossed a cocktail weenie into his mouth, tapped the top of the cage next to him — marked SQUIRRELS FOR SALE — and leered at us. Service with a smile, right?

"Hi, uh, excuse me," Eric said cautiously. "You work here?"

"No, I'm just out here 'cause I like it," he snarled at us. "Just had the exterminator here. Had roaches the size of a small child running around in there."

"How much for a room?" Eric asked. Was he crazy? No way were we staying here. No way.

"Fifty an hour," the clerk said. "Or seventy-nine per room for the whole night."

"Be right back." Eric pulled us into a huddle. No one said anything; we all just stared at one another. And then, slowly, I realized — everyone else was staring at me. No way. Not my money, not for a roach-infested hole like this. Not in a million years.

"No way!"

"C'mon, man," Eric wheedled. "It's an investment."

"In us," Matt added.

"Hey, I have an idea," I said. "Why don't I throw my cash directly into the toilet and flush?" I laughed, but no one else did. Too bad. I wasn't budging on this one. "I can't do it."

"You can," Eric said.

"I can't."

"You *can*."

"I can't." More importantly, I *won't*, which is what I was about to say when Eric suddenly got that look in his eyes. You know the one.

He held up his hand. "Hold on . . ."

Eric went back over to the bell clerk. "How 'bout we clean your pool and you let us stay here tonight?"

The bell clerk couldn't believe what he was hearing (neither could we). "You're saying you're gonna clean that toxic mess?"

Eric nodded confidently. "Absolutely."

The bell clerk laughed and laughed, and tossed a room key to Eric. "You do the deed and Room 126 is yours."

Matt

The pool was total gnarly nastiness, but my boy Eric had a raging plan. No, dude — he had a vision. And once we cleared the junk out of the pool, we saw it, too. This was no ordinary gnarly motel pool. This was the perfect place for a perfect skate session.

We pulled out our boards, flipped on the video camera, and kicked it all afternoon — old school.

It. Was. Awesome.

Dustin

So okay. I admit it. Cleaning the pool wasn't *that* horrendous, once we got the junk out of the way and grabbed our boards. And, to be honest, grindin' the pool was even kind of fun — not that I'd ever admit that out loud.

So we cleaned the pool, got our gross free room, and spread out for sleep. At least there was a bed. Or actually, a heart-shaped bed — we were in the honeymoon suite. I stuck to Eric like glue — no way was I lyin' down next to Matt or Sweet Lou.

I lay there for hours in the darkness, staring at the ceiling, too nervous, or uncomfortable, or bored to sleep. Finally, I couldn't take it anymore.

"You awake?" I whispered to Eric.

"I'm just lying here waiting for the next bug to try and bite me," he whispered back.

I wanted to ask him something — but I didn't want to ask. I think I was afraid of his answer. But lying awake in the middle of the night waiting for cockroaches to attack can make you do strange things. So I said it. "You really think we have a chance?"

"Totally," Eric said, and you could tell he really felt it. "We were meant to do this, Dustin. Everyone has something they're good at." He paused. "I want to be the best at this."

We lay there in silence for a minute, thinking. I knew that deep down, he really was convinced that this whole trip was the right thing to do — that despite all we'd been through, everything was going to work out.

And the weird thing was, I was starting to believe him.

Eric

Okay, so we'd hit a few bumps on our path to success. But things were finally getting into gear. We were back on the road, grooving to some awesome music, watching the country flow by, and speeding toward our destiny. Well, right now were were on the side of the road, taking a leak, but we'd be speeding toward our destiny soon. And the guys were finally getting the right attitude — even Dustin. Sort of.

"I am just so psyched to be skating this summer instead of Mc-Jobbin' it," I said — and no matter what happened next, it couldn't be worse than spending the summer behind the counter at Chili 'N' Such.

"Two scoops cheddar, one scoop onions," Dustin joked, imitating Cameron's smarmy style.

"You're makin' me hungry," Sweet Lou complained. And, as if it had heard him, my stomach growled like a wild beast. How long had it been since we'd eaten?

"Dusty, we got enough allowance to cop some food?" I asked. "We're starving."

"No way." Dustin shook his head furiously. "I draw the line. The line is drawn."

Dustin's kind of a tightwad, but I can usually get him to shell it out a little — the dude knows what's really important.

"We need your help, dude," I said. "Short-term. We'll pay you back."

I was just getting started, but Sweet Lou didn't understand the subtle approach. "Come on, man," he whined. "I'm so hungry, I think I'm actually starving to death. Right now. Do something!"

Dustin put his hands on his hips and shook his head again. "I can't do it."

"You can," I told him. This always works.

"I can't."

"You can."

"I *can't*."

Okay . . . so, like I said, Dustin's a total tightwad and we don't need his money anyway. There's always room for a Plan B. If I could just come up with one . . .

ᴥᴥᴥᴥᴥ

We drove and drove until we spotted a Chili 'N' Such on the side of the road. If we couldn't *buy* food, we'd have to scam some — and who better to scam than our beloved former employers, the great men and women of Chili 'N' Such.

Dustin and I kicked it into gear.

"You know the drill," I said, getting into the driver's seat.

"Oh yeah." Dustin hopped out of the van and took off.

"What?" Sweet Lou asked. "What're you doing? We don't have any cash!"

Patience, patience — you'll see soon enough.

Dustin

The things I do for friendship. And hunger.

I trolled the front of the Chili 'N' Such, searching the gutter until I found exactly what I needed. Some kid was standing close by — *too close* — watching me, and it was creeping me out. Finally, he got up enough nerve to say something.

"What're you doing?"

"I dropped something," I said. "I'm looking for it."

The kid grinned up at me. "I had curly cheese fries. Lots of them. And a chocolate shake."

"Didn't your mother ever tell you not to talk to strangers?" I asked. What was wrong with this kid?

I was about to find out.

He looked up at me, opened his mouth like he was about to say something, then made the most disgusting noise I've ever heard — and threw up. All over me.

Dude.

The kid ran away crying for his mother — and standing there dripping with vomit, I wished I could do that, too.

It's now or never: Sweet Lou, Matt, Dustin, and Eric are determined to become pro skaters.

Road ready: the Super Duper Skateboarders van.

Livin' the dream: Eric with his board.

Every road has a few speed bumps —
the guys have to do a little grunt work
along the way.

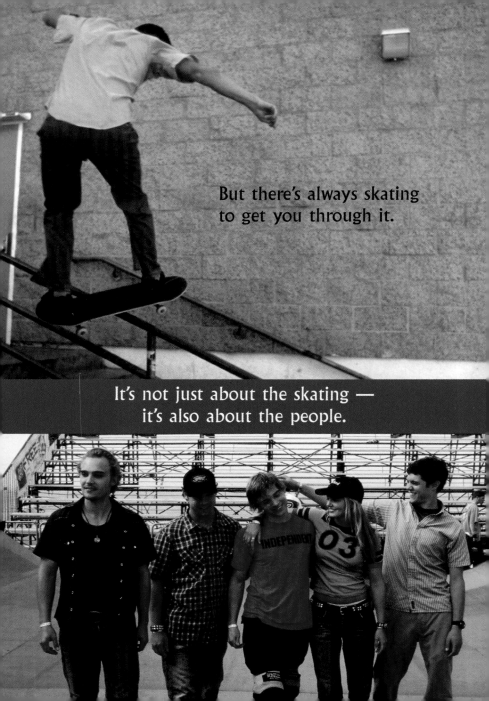

But there's always skating
to get you through it.

It's not just about the skating —
it's also about the people.

A pro demo.

Eric finally gets his big shot...

...while his buds cheer him on.

At the end of the day, you just gotta believe...
in your friends, and in yourself.

But what was that floating in the pool of half-digested curly cheese fries? Could it be what I was looking for?

Oh, gross. No way am I sticking my hand in there. No way. No way.

The things I do for friendship. And hunger.

❧❧❧❧❧

I went over to the driver's side of the van and handed Eric the receipt — it was still dripping.

"Ew, dude," he complained. I don't know what he was whining about — I was the one that had to go digging for buried treasure!

I just shrugged my shoulders and said, "Best I could do." But it better have been worth it.

Eric pulled into the drive-through and leaned out toward the speaker. "Listen, I came by about an hour ago and ordered ten of the gut bomb chili surprises and five shakes and when I got home, all that was in the bag was some coffee that was superhot and I spilled it on myself and I'm horribly burned. . . ."

The guy on the other end of the drive-through speaker sounded shocked. "Sir, was that ten chili surprises and five shakes?"

"Yes. Chocolate shakes. I've got the receipt right here."

The drive-through guy totally bought it. "I remember that order. Drive through and we'll replace it. Chili 'N' Such is in the customer service business and we're sorry for this inconvenience."

Score! We'd actually done it — I knew that customer service junk would come in handy sometime. I said a silent prayer of thanks to Cameron for teaching me how pathetic the Chili 'N' Such staff could be, then grabbed my chili surprise and my chocolate shake.

Now if I could only get back my appetite . . .

Eric

It seemed like we'd been driving for years. But it all seemed worth it when we pulled into the Colorado skate shop lot. And I wasn't the only one who thought so.

"Dude, this is the most famous skate shop in Colorado," Matt said, impressed. "This is where Jimmy Wilson got discovered."

And today, Jimmy Wilson was going to discover *us*. We'd been waiting long enough.

"Where's Jimmy's bus?" Dustin asked, looking around. "There should be a big crowd here."

Matt looked confused. "Maybe we're early?"

We all shrugged, then got out of the van to check out the skate shop. If we were early, we could at least kill some time checking out some killer gear.

"We're here to check out the Jimmy Wilson demo," I told the guy behind the counter.

"It was really something," he said.

Was?

"What day is it?" Dustin asked, starting to get upset. "It's Saturday, right?"

The skate shop owner gave us a funny look. "It's Sunday. They were here yesterday."

Matt didn't get it. "It happened already?"

"That is what 'yesterday' means," the guy said, looking disgusted.

"Great." Dustin turned around, ready to walk out. "We lost a day!"

Dustin's my best friend, but he's such a downer sometimes. He never sees the positive possibilities of a situation. I mean, yeah, so we'd screwed up. We'd missed Jimmy, and we were stuck in the middle of nowhere with nothing to do. But was that the worst thing that could happen?

"Let's look on the bright side," I said. "Maybe we can demo here." I turned to the skate shop owner. "We're the Super Duper Skateboard team. You think it'd be okay to cone off a section of your parking lot?"

"Sure, man," he said.

Matt

Man, move over, Sweet Lou, there's a new master in town. This guy was brilliant! I had a new life plan. If the whole pro skating thing didn't work out, I'd just follow in his footsteps. Put together a little skate museum of my own. I could start right now. Yeah. I'd just start collecting all my used Band-Aids. And Eric and Dustin have all kinds of scabs and snot and good stuff like that. Sweet.

So I could've stayed in the magic room all day, but Eric wanted to skate. Kid's got a total one-track mind, know what I mean?

We coned off the parking lot — the dude would only give us enough space for one little fun box.

"A great skater can make something out of nothing," he said. "Take this concrete nothingness and make something happen."

Dude, this dude was like a genius or something.

We put on a raging demo. Some kids even showed up to cheer us on. I shot some killer video of Eric — he didn't even make me turn it off when this snot-nosed kid started raggin' on him.

"Dude, you're pretty good," this kid says.

Eric stopped skating. "Thanks."

And then the kid says, "But I could totally take you. You're not even trying to bring it."

Eric was gettin' steamed. "You saying I don't risk it? What grade are you in?"

"Seventh. I'm twelve. And a half."

Eric couldn't believe it. "And you've got something to teach me? Talk to me when your voice changes."

I guess the puny punk didn't want to wait that long. He grabbed his board and started a demo of his own. And he was good — I mean, he was the real deal. Eric looked like someone spit in his soup.

I was gonna go over there and teach that kid some respect for his elders . . . but I got distracted.

Sweet Lou had found himself another sweet lady.

And she was hot.

I leaned back to watch the old master in action.

"What's up?" he drawled.

"You," the skate chick said, popping her gum.

"Nice. You want me?"

"Yeah." She grabbed his hand and they took off.

Dude's a genius.

Dustin

So Eric was living his dream, getting his own pro skate demo and his own screaming fans. I was happy for him and all, but back here on Earth, the natives were getting restless.

And by "natives," I mean snot-nosed kids with food all over their faces and a nasty, greedy gleam in their eyes.

"When's the product toss?" one shouted.

"We want some free stuff!" called out another — and I was getting a little worried about what would happen when we couldn't deliver. These kids looked *mean*.

"If you losers are really sponsored, where's the free stuff?"

They started creeping toward me — and I wasn't the only one. That kid who'd been fronting to Eric had discovered Sweet Lou and was getting all in his face about finding some babes. Even Eric got knocked out of fantasy land when some kid rolled up to him demanding, "Gimme a free shirt. Gimme your wallet. Gimme your shoes."

They may have been smaller than us, but there were a lot of them — and they were vicious. Matt grabbed his board out of their hands, knocking one down to the pavement. Score one for us!

But whenever we got rid of one, five more showed up. Where were they all coming from?

Still, they were just kids. Not a huge problem —

Uh-oh.

Now they were kids with tire irons. Kids with tire irons trying to steal the wheels off our van.

Suddenly, they rushed us, and we pushed our way into the van.

"These brats want blood!" Sweet Lou panted, finally safe inside the van.

The punks threw themselves up against the sides of the van, trying to get in, shouting and taunting us.

"Your team sucks!"

It was still ringing in my ears as we sped away.

Eric

Dude, that was a close one.

But we got away — and hey, whatever else happened, I still got my first pro demo, right?

So now we were back on the road, just the five of us. Me, Dustin, Matt, Sweet Lou . . . and Sweet Lou's new "friend." The girl he'd picked up back at the skate shop. Let me tell you, you've never really driven until you've driven with someone who's steering and making out with his girlfriend. At the same time.

And then just when things were going really well —

Okay, just when things were going about as badly as they could, they got worse.

The tire blew out, and the van swerved off the road.

Great. Just great.

We piled out of the van and, since Dustin drew the short straw (story of his life, if you ask him), he got to work fixing the tire. Sweet Lou stayed inside the van with his honey. And Matt and me? We waited.

"How do we get Jimmy to see us if we can't even skate a contest?" Matt complained.

"And the Betties have been totally scarce," Dustin added.

"Whaddya mean?" I asked. "They're everywhere!" Or at least, they're inside our van with Sweet Lou. I pointed over to the happy couple.

"And that's another thing," Matt said. "Sweet Lou brought that girl along!"

"Why does that bother you?" I asked.

" 'Cause it's not happening to me!"

I should have guessed. Matt's got, shall we say, terrible luck with the ladies.

"If you would change your clothes even one time," Dustin suggested. "I swear, we should bungee him to the roof of the van to air him out."

Dustin

The days lasted forever. I didn't even remember what state we were in anymore. All I knew is we were parked on the side of the road in Nowhereville, trying not to get cooked by the heat. We all needed a break from the van — it was driving us insane to be cooped up together in such a small space. Not that being outside was helping. I could still barely stand the sight of any of them. I guess Sweet Lou's new girl felt the same way, since she was still holed up in the van. I looked over at Eric, who was still grinning that stupid grin of his. I wanted to smack it off his face.

"All I know is that we've been following your lead on this since forever," I said, "and you've kept us going by completely gutting my college fund!"

Eric just kept smiling. "This is what separates the men from the boys."

"You mean those boys who beat us up at that pathetic excuse of a demo?" Sweet Lou asked.

That was it — I couldn't take it anymore. It was time for some kind of action. Any action. I jumped up. "If we get back now, maybe I can save my job. Two scoops cheddar, one scoop onion." Suddenly, it sounded like a magical combination.

They just ignored me — it's like I don't even exist on this trip! Unless they need my money — then it's, "Oh, Dustin, save us, Dustin, be a part of the team, Dustin."

But for now they just ignored me.

Sweet Lou was making a ketchup sandwich. By which I mean he was smearing fast-food ketchup packets onto some white bread. Yum. Eric, meanwhile, was gobbling down sugar packets.

"The good news is that it's all uphill from here." He paused to scarf more sugar. "It can't get any worse." (Now, when does saying those words *not* make something worse happen? Has Eric never seen a movie? As soon as he opened his mouth, I knew it was only a matter of time before disaster struck.)

Matt didn't even have sugar. He just kept searching through the empty food bag and coming up — you guessed it — empty.

And me? I had my very real, very delicious meat-filled sandwich. Is it a crime that I used *my* money to buy myself some food? So sue me.

They looked at me like they wanted to do worse than that.

"What?" I asked grumpily. "You're trying to guilt me out over the fact that I've worked hard and saved some money and with that money I've bought myself some food?"

It sounded reasonable to me. I was totally in the right. I was congratulating myself for not being a hungry, moneyless loser like the rest of these guys when Matt reached over, snatched the sandwich out of my hands, and shoved it into his mouth. All at once. Every last bit. Seriously.

I just looked at him.

"What?" he asked, around a mouthful of *my* food.

It was just pathetic. "You're a massive jerk," I told him. There was no more food — there was just my empty stomach and the hot desert sun. Great.

At least things couldn't get any —

Oh no.

We all looked up at the sound of an engine roaring — our engine. And with that, the van pulled away, Sweet Lou's skater chick at the wheel. I couldn't believe it.

We took off running after the van.

"Wait up!" I called. But it was no use.

"I said no girls," Matt said accusingly.

We shuffled over to where the van had been parked — all our stuff was piled on the ground.

"At least she left our stuff," Eric said.

Somehow, that didn't cheer me up. I know I can be a little quick to judge a situation, I know I'm sometimes a little quick to panic — but have you ever heard of a better time to panic? "We're stranded!" I shouted, trying to break through Eric's freakish calm. "What're we gonna do? We've got no money, no wheels, no team." I paused. "No hope."

Eric refused to get beaten down. "We need some kind of sign, something to tell us to keep going," he said. "That we haven't lost our skate karma."

No one answered. Maybe they were all thinking what I was thinking, which was that we lost our skate karma the moment we made a deal with the devil — excuse me, Sweet Lou — and piled into his van. The moment we decided to go on this stupid trip in the first place.

Eric was looking down at the ground, waiting for someone else to speak first. When no one did, he looked up again, determined. "No! This dream does not end in the middle of ten-thousand-degree Nowhereville with us beaten like dirty, smelly, broken dogs."

Uh, Eric, I beg to differ, but it seems that's exactly where the dream has ended. What would it take to knock some sense into this guy?

"Yeah, I'm sure the great Jimmy Wilson is gonna give us a deal," I said mockingly. "Wait. I see his bus now, he's coming back to get us! We're saved! Oh, sorry, it's a mirage." By this point I was shouting in Eric's face. "'Cause we're in the middle of the desert!"

Maybe it sounds a little harsh. But I really thought it was the right thing to do. After all, there we were in the middle of the desert with no hope and a pile of junk to our name, and Eric was still expecting his hero to appear over the horizon and sweep us away to our destiny. I felt that it was my duty, as his best friend, to make him understand that he was wrong and I was right.

And I was absolutely sure I was right.

Until we heard a rumble.

Saw a cloud of exhaust.

And Jimmy Wilson's tour bus pulled up beside us.

Eric

Okay, so the bus didn't stop. But it had to be a sign. It was meant to be. *This* was meant to be. And I mean there was an actual sign — it read NEXT STOP TUCSON — and so that's exactly where we were headed.

We ran after the bus, but it didn't stop. No matter — we'd catch up with them eventually. I just knew it, deep down at my core: Everything was gonna work out.

ରରରରର

So we threw our stuff into some garbage bags, grabbed our boards, and we walked.

And walked.

And walked.

Through totally deserted streets, through a countryside that looked like a desert wasteland.

And we walked some more.

"Yeah, I think I see your sign up ahead," Dustin said, a few hours into the hike. "It says, 'We're all doomed.'"

"Don't forget we have no water," Sweet Lou added. As if any of us could forget that.

"I think I'm having an aneurysm," Dustin complained.

I was sick of the whining, I was sick of the walking — and, to be honest, I was pretty thirsty myself.

"Just keep your eyes on the road," I said. And that's exactly what we did.

Matt

So tired.

So hungry.

So thirsty.

So cold.

And, to top it all off, I'd almost fallen asleep when some slimy thing started shimmying around in my pants. A lizard. Great.

Dude, road trips are rough when you don't have a van. Or a motel room. Or a pillow.

Dustin had a pillow — and I figured, since we were all sleeping together on the ground, and since we were supposed to be a team and all, he wouldn't mind if I borrowed it. Just for a little nap.

So I grabbed it away. Oh, and then I rubbed it under my pits. That should keep the rest of these vultures away from it for the night.

"Quit it," Dustin whined. "That's my special pillow."

Tough.

I was just dropping off to sleep when I heard it. A coyote howl.

"No one's food here!" Eric yelled into the darkness.

I closed my eyes, hoping it would decide to eat the smelly guy last.

Dustin

More walking, with no end in sight. I was sick of the walking, I was sick of the outdoors — I was even getting sick of complaining (and for me, that's a first). We all felt it. This couldn't go on forever.

"We need some cash," Eric said. "It's end-of-the-line desperate." And, surprise, surprise, he was looking at me.

"No no no no no no. I can't," I said. "There is no more. That's it. All gone." And it was true. I wasn't holding out on them anymore. We'd eaten, driven, and slept through my entire college fund — and look where it'd gotten us.

"Okay," Eric said, looking into the distance. "I'll think of something."

❧❧❧❧❧

So it came to this. Sweet Lou, standing shirtless on the side of the road with his thumb out.

And it worked.

A gorgeous Native American chick rolled to a stop in her RV, and Sweet Lou hadn't said two words before she invited us all to pile in.

As we drove along, Matt suddenly let out a shriek. "Uh, guys?" Matt pointed behind us.

We turned around to face a huge billboard advertising — you won't believe this one — the JIMMY WILSON TEAM SKATE EVENT, happening that very day, in that very place.

How does Eric do it? I mean, every time! *How does he do it?*

Matt

We were at this pro skate for about five minutes before Sweet Lou already had each arm wrapped around a different girl.

How did this guy do it? I'd been hanging around him forever, watching him, waiting for lightning to strike, and I was still totally clueless.

Enough was enough.

I walked up to Sweet Lou and the hot honeys. "Hi."

The hotter one actually spoke to me. You could tell she didn't want to, but hey, she did it anyway. "How's it goin'?"

"For me, not so good. See, I need to ask you girls —" Deep breath. Chill, Matt. Chill. "What's wrong with me?"

The girl wrinkled her nose. I get that a lot. "In what way?"

"I mean, why can't I ever get a girl? What's wrong with me?" I showed her some of my moves. "I'm crazy! I'm edgy! I can be a bad, bad boy. . . ."

The girl turned to Sweet Lou. "He's with you?"

Sweet Lou wouldn't even look at me. "Not anymore."

So I'd offended the master. So what? I couldn't take it anymore. "I really need to know. What could I do that would make a girl like me?" I begged. "Whatever it is, I'll do it."

The girl thought for a second.

This was it. I was finally going to get some useful info.

"Well . . . you could go away," she said.

Eric

Not another security guy. And this one looked just as cranky as all the rest. Was there a factory somewhere that mass-produced these guys — big, angry men whose sole purpose was to crush the dreams of young skateboarders all over the world?

Doubtful. But I was getting sick of running into them. I needed to get backstage to see Jimmy, which means I needed to find a way around this guy. I put on my biggest, brightest smile.

"Hey, what's up, man?"

The security guy nodded. So far, so good. And then, someone caught my eye — someone way more important than security dude.

"Hey, Bam!" I called out to him. "How's the tour going?" A pro skater from my hometown. From my home skate shop. If I could get in with him, maybe he could get me backstage.

"Sheer insanity," Bam said. "I remember you." He remembered me? *He* remembered *me*? Score! "What's up?"

Bam sailed through security — that's fame and success for you. I tried to follow him, but the guard stuck out a meaty hand and stopped me in my tracks.

"He's with me," Bam said.

I was with him! I looked at the security guard like, Hey, dude, looks like you didn't know who you were dealing with. Then caught up with my new buddy Bam. I had to seize this opportunity — and hey, there's no time like the present, right?

"Actually, if you have a minute, I'd really like to talk to you." I was talking as fast as I could to get it all out before he could stop me. "Show you some video, maybe you could pass it on to Jimmy. . . ."

"No problem," Bam said, grinning.

Did I really just hear that? Am I dreaming?

And it just kept getting better. A moment later, the girl of my dreams walked back into my life and right up to us. I looked at the two of them, imagining the future — my new best friend and my new best girl, all three of us living happily ever after. . . .

"If you're gonna talk behind my back, Bam, at least be man enough to say it to my face," she snarled, breaking into my daydream.

Uh, maybe we wouldn't be the happy trio after all?

"If you *are* man enough, that is," she continued.

Bam got up in her face. "I don't want you around. And it's not just me. You're hurtin' the vibe."

She wasn't taking any of that. "But I *am* here. Deal with it." Man, she was beautiful when she was mad. "And what I don't need to be around is you and your lame friends!"

"What we don't need on this tour is the smell of a rank female!" Chad shouted.

Now right here, I had a choice.

Play it smart and keep quiet, be a silent supporter of my new buddy Bam — and finally make it to the pros. Become a world-famous skateboarder. Be famous, rich, and happy forever.

Or, I could stick up for this girl I'd never spoken more than two words in a row to, just because I thought she had cute hair.

It was a no-brainer.

"Whoa, bud. That is not cool," I told Bam. "I think you should apologize."

He turned on me in an instant. "What was that?"

"You heard what I said." I was trying to sound tough, even though I was quaking inside. "Apologize."

And, wonder of wonders, Bam actually backed down. "Later for you," he said, turning away. "Both of you."

I had escaped a beating — but the churning sound of my dreams getting flushed down the toilet was echoing in my ears.

Then I turned to look at Her. And suddenly, I wasn't so miserable anymore. I wasn't miserable at all, actually.

"Thanks," she said.

I tried to brush it off. "He was out of line."

"But I think I can take care of myself," she said, all tough. God, she was beautiful when she was acting tough.

"Never hurts to have someone backin' you up," I said, smiling, hoping it was the right thing.

Bingo.

She smiled. "Wanna take a walk?"

And I could have died happy.

Dustin

Oh, this was not a good idea. Not a good idea. You know that little voice in your head that tells you when you shouldn't be doing something? Well, it was screaming — "Get out! Get out! Get out!" But did I listen?

Let's be honest, I stopped listening to that little voice a long time ago. If I hadn't, I would be safe on the couch, watching TV after a nice long day at Chili 'N' Such. Instead, here I was with Matt, pulling a Mission Impossible in Jimmy Wilson's tour bus.

Were we going to get caught? Oh, that seemed inevitable. But by this point, I'd pretty much given up on ever doing the smart thing again. So why not just let Matt be in charge?

He poked his head through the door. "Hello? Anyone home?"

No answer. "Don't touch anything!" I warned him. "We're gonna get busted!"

He jumped on the bus, and I followed behind him. Did I mention this was so not a good idea? But dude, I had to admit — how cool was this? We were on Jimmy Wilson's tour bus!

Okay, focus.

"We've got the place to ourselves," Matt said. "I wonder what's in the fridge." He checked inside, pulled out a giant piece of chicken, and took a bite. Then stuffed the rest in his pocket.

I ignored him. Sometimes with Matt, that's all you can do.

I picked up a copy of the latest *Transworld*, and leafed through it. And then I realized — Jimmy Wilson was on the cover. And how weird — here we were in his bus.

"So near greatness," I murmured to myself. And it was totally greatness. Jimmy had the bus tricked out like he was a rock star — couches, entertainment center, full kitchen — I'm sure there was a hot tub back there somewhere.

Matt, of course, headed right from the fridge to the bathroom. "Thank the lord," he said. "I've been holding it in for, like, two days."

Like I said, ignore him.

Well, we'd made it in. Now it was time to get to work. I pulled out our tour video — the record of all the "conquests" from our summer adventure — and stuck it in the camcorder. Just a little stealth mission. Picture it: Jimmy gets on the bus, grabs the camcorder, and *bam*! Our tape'll be in the machine, he'll see it, and we'll be on our way —

That was the theory, anyway.

And then the tape got caught in the camcorder. And started unraveling. I tried to pull it out, but it was no good. It was stuck.

And that's when I heard the voices.

Matt popped out of the bathroom. He'd been in there *way* too long — if you know what I mean. "Someone's coming! Hide!"

We ducked out of sight, and just in time. Jimmy Wilson and another skate pro stepped onto the bus.

"I still can't believe you landed that," the pro said.

"Highest air ever achieved by a man on a board," Jimmy said, sounding pretty proud of himself. "And I've got the video to prove it!"

There was a pause. I couldn't see anything, but I figured he'd just spotted the mess I'd made of his machine. Oops.

The other pro groaned. "Tell me that's not your only copy."

There was another pause, and now I figured they had both just caught a whiff of the stench wafting out of the bathroom.

"Crack a window," the pro pleaded.

"I need some air," Jimmy choked out — and they both ran off the bus.

Not a moment too soon. Matt and I burst out of the bathroom, ready to pass out ourselves. We stumbled off the bus.

Mission accomplished.

Sort of.

Eric

Her name was Jamie, and she was wonderful. Even better than I'd expected. She had somehow managed to get me in backstage, and on the way, I'd told her our whole story. I'd never met anyone so easy to talk to — especially not a girl!

". . . so we've basically been chasin' the Jimmy Wilson tour across the country for the past two weeks," I told her.

"That's pretty crazy," she said.

"Yeah. I thought if I could get him to really watch us skating, he'd pick us up." Now that I was saying it out loud to a beautiful stranger, it sounded kind of, well, stupid. "But we totally screwed everything up. Basically, our whole tour's been a complete disaster. . . ." I paused, not wanting to scare her away. But she seemed worth the chance. "Until now."

"Now?"

I blushed. "Yeah. You know, the 'talking to you' part."

And, giant sigh of relief, she actually smiled. "Right. So, do you have a Plan B?"

Plan B? I love this girl!

"Well, I did," I admitted, "but now Bam thinks I'm a tool."

She looked embarrassed. "Thanks for standing up for me."

Just thinking about it made me remember how much I'd lost. "He was, like, this close to checkin' out my tape!" I paused. "But hey, he was acting like a jerk. So . . . were you into him?"

Jamie recoiled at the thought. "Bam? You think I'm into him 'cause he's on tour?"

Did I say something wrong? It made sense to me. "Aren't you into the pros and that whole world?" I asked.

Now she looked mad. What'd I say? "Yeah, sure," she said sarcastically. "Any pro can have me. You've got me pegged."

"I don't mean anything by it," I said, talking fast, trying to smooth things over. "I think you're supercute. You're the cutest girl I've met on tour. I'd throw myself under the wheels of Jimmy Wilson's bus so I could land a girl like you." I stopped to take a breath, and she jumped in.

"It's you and your skateboard and what you make of it that'll get you where you want to go," she said, looking serious. "It's not who you brownnose."

I sighed. It seemed hopeless. "It's like I'm on the outside looking in."

She moved in closer, put out a hand like she was going to comfort me, then stopped. "Keep skating, and someone will find you," she said. Things still seemed hopeless, but it was nice of her to try. "Cream rises to the top. I know about these things."

We were both quiet for a minute, just looking into each other's eyes. I was trying to get up the nerve to kiss her. I took a deep breath and —

"Dude, we were so close!" Dustin suddenly appeared by my side, with Matt close behind him. I snapped out of it — what was I thinking, focusing on romance when we had a destiny to pursue?

"You got on the bus?" I asked eagerly.

Matt nodded. "He was, like, right there."

Things were turning around, I could feel it. I glanced over at an ATV in the parking lot, and suddenly, I had another idea. A brilliant idea. An idea that would jerk us out of this rut and into the rock-star, skater-stud life of Jimmy Wilson.

"Dude, I know how to pull this off," I said. "I'm gonna bust out my dream trick — the three-sixty flip over the hip. He'll see it and have to sign us up."

Dustin looked doubtful. As always. "I don't know," he said. "You've never landed it."

Maybe not, but what does that mean? "This is my one chance," I said firmly. This time, I wasn't messing up. I turned to Jamie. "We've got some serious skating to do. I'll catch up with you."

And we left Jamie behind and headed out to meet our destiny.

❧❧❧❧❧

We staked out Jimmy Wilson's bus, which was parked out in the lot next to a bunch of Porta Potties. It was dark and empty, but I knew he'd have to come back eventually. And when Jimmy and his crew showed up, I'd show them my stuff, and they'd have to let us on the tour.

So we waited.

92

And waited.

And, just as we'd all dropped off to sleep (waiting is hard work), the bus horn blared. The bus was moving out!

I scrambled up — I had to catch them before they left. I grabbed my board and waited for Dustin to start up the ATV — I would have to land this trick at the perfect moment.

"Ready, hold on." Dustin held up his hand. "Hold on . . . Now!"

The ATV was cruising in front of the bus — with me in tow! It was now or never. I took a deep breath, and went for it! The backside 360 flip over the hip — and as I was spinning through the air, I could feel it. It was perfect. This time, I was going to land it, solid.

I could hear the guys cheering, and I knew we'd finally done it. And then I saw the bus — it had made a sharp right before it got to me. They totally missed my trick.

I hadn't impressed Jimmy Wilson. He wouldn't invite me on his tour. It was over.

I turned back to watch the bus disappear into the distance, but my board was still going forward — and it took me with it, right into a Porta Potti. I crashed to the ground, and so did the Porta Potti, along with all the rest in that row, like a line of dominoes.

I lay on the ground, totally defeated.

"They're not stopping!" Dustin cried, waving his hands at the vanishing bus.

Matt shook his head. "He didn't see it."

"But I did."

I looked up at the owner of the deep voice. A big guy. A big, angry guy.

Oh no . . . not another security guard.

"And I'm sick and tired of you punks thinkin' you can skate any-where you feel like!"

"But we're at a skating event," Dustin pointed out.

The big dude pointed to a sign. It read NO SKATING. Uh-oh.

"Someone's gotta teach you people some sense," he thundered. "I could have you arrested, but for once, you skaters are gonna clean up your own mess."

I did *not* like the sound of that.

He pointed to the row of tipped-over Porta Potties. And stood there and grinned as we miserably got to work.

Dustin

I take it all back. Did I say this trip was horrible before? Did I say this trip was a nightmare? I don't know what I was thinking — because I didn't even know the meaning of the words *horrible nightmare* until five minutes ago. I didn't realize that sleeping in the desert with no food, no water, no protection, and Matt lying on top of me drooling was like a day at the beach compared to what life just dropped in our laps.

We stumbled away from the Porta Potties, filthy, angry, and totally exhausted. "So, to recap, we smell like turds," I pointed out. "We have no wheels. And no Jimmy Wilson." Need I go on? How about it. "I'm broke and I guess you can call me stupid. Thank you, Eric."

Eric didn't say anything. Well, that's got to be a first.

"C'mon," Matt said. "Aren't you gonna look on the bright side of this like you always do?" He imitated Eric's "inspirational" tone: "It's just a glitch on the road to skating glory. . . ."

Eric still said nothing. I was starting to worry. This wasn't like him.

"Say something!" Sweet Lou begged.

Nothing.

"You're scaring us!" I said. Even lame motivational speeches would be better than this.

He'd clearly hit the breaking point. You could see something building up inside of him. And then, it all just came pouring out.

"What do you want me to say? That I've been living in a dreamworld? A world where a loser like me has a chance to get on a tour with Jimmy Wilson?"

I couldn't stand to hear him talk that way. Not Eric. "Don't say that," I said.

"Why not? It's true, isn't it? What am I doing out here? I'm pathetic. I mean, I'm, like, one step away from being a stalker, for crying out loud!" I didn't know what to do — what if he burst into tears? He looked kinda like he wanted to. I mean, guys just aren't equipped for this sort of thing. So I just listened. "I let you guys down. I should never have gotten your hopes up in the first place."

And then, of all people, Sweet Lou opened his mouth. And said the first intelligent thing I've ever heard come out of it. "Let's get one thing straight, Eric. We all followed you out here because you got passion. You got nerve. And I hope this road trip never ends, 'cause I'm having the best time I've ever had!"

After all we'd been through, it was ridiculous. But bizarrely, it was also true.

"I'm actually having fun," I admitted. "Real fun. I feel alive."

"You got us out here, man," Matt chimed in. "We're having an adventure, dude."

And suddenly, we were all back on top of the world — all except Eric.

He looked down at the ground, refusing to meet our eyes. "No. What we're having is a hapless nightmare stuck on an endless loop, destined to repeat failure after failure."

We had to snap him out of it — this team needed its leader. We needed Eric.

"We've seen some great things," Sweet Lou said. "We've done some awesome skating. And we owe it all to you. You know that!"

"Yeah, man," Matt added. "Remember what you said. We're a team."

Eric still didn't answer. But I thought I caught a hint of a smile.

Eric

I appreciated the guys trying to cheer me up, but I still didn't know where to go from here. As far as I could tell, our trip was all washed up. I looked up at the security guard, who was just standing there laughing at us, as if he knew exactly what was up and thought it was the funniest thing he'd ever heard.

Then Dustin actually stepped up and told the dude to shut it! Even your best friends can surprise you sometimes, I guess.

"We did your work, mister," he said. "And now we're going to catch up to Jimmy Wilson wherever he's skating next. . . ."

And then a beautiful voice gave us the answer to our prayers.

"Oceanside. It's the last stop on his tour." It was Jamie — and suddenly, life seemed a little brighter. "It's the last stop on the contest circuit for the season. And it's an open pro jam."

"Open pro jam?" I repeated. This sounded promising.

"Yeah, if you're a pro or sponsored skater, you can ride." She grinned. "So . . . you were trying to land the three-sixty flip over the hip back there?"

"I'm *going* to land it," I said, with new resolve.

"I could try to help you out," she offered, "maybe go with you. . . ."

Just as I was about to cry, "Yes! Yes! Yes!" Matt interrupted.

"Team meeting!" he shouted, pulling us into a huddle.

I knew what he was thinking, but Jamie was no thieving skater chick. "She's a really great girl," I said.

But Matt was staying firm. "No females on tour."

"Remember what happened to the van," Dustin said. Then he looked thoughtful. "Does she have a vehicle? We're kind of stranded."

Matt shook his head violently. "No extra baggage. We gotta run lean and mean."

Jamie interrupted us. "I can hear you guys — I'm right over here."

Are we idiots, or what?

But fortunately, Jamie once again proved what an awesome girl she was. "It's cool," she said. "I don't want to cramp your style. I hope you make it out to the beach." Then she looked into my eyes and smiled. "You have something special. You just won't give up. Just don't forget why you're skating in the first place."

I couldn't tear myself away from her. "Jamie —" I started. And then stopped. I didn't know what to say.

"Keep skating, Eric. I'll see ya." And she turned and walked away.

Would I ever see her again?

Matt

It got heavy there for a while, but things were righteous again.

Of course, we still had no wheels.

But a little walking never hurt anyone, right?

"Eric, are you back with us?" Sweet Lou asked. He didn't have to — it was obvious to all of us that all Eric had needed was a little heads up from his little honey. Now he was totally back on his game.

"Sorry about the mini freak show back there," he said. "I'll try not to screw up worse than I already have."

Bad choice of words, dude. That just made us think of everything that was still wrong. Like the whole no wheels thing. Or the no bed thing. Or the no food thing.

"I'm starving," Dustin complained — talk about a whiner. "I think one of my ribs is breaking through the skin."

Sweet Lou got a dangerous look in his eyes. "I would literally kill for a night in a real bed."

We're talking crisis situation here. And little did they know it, but I had the answer to their problems.

Could I help? Was I strong enough?

I had to search my soul — I mean, dude, I really had to dig deep. It was a big decision. What if I totally lost their respect?

I looked at the guys, at my bros, my team, and that's when I knew. I had to step up to the plate, set my feet on the board.

"All right," I said, determined. "It's time to meet the clowns."

Dustin

I thought Matt was using some sort of metaphor — which, admittedly, would have been a first for him — but no. When he said "meet the clowns," that's exactly what he meant.

He took us to a small building with a couple guys out front on lawn chairs, reading the paper. Sounds normal, right? Except that the guys were wearing clown makeup. And the sign next to them read JENSENS' CLOWN SCHOOL.

I looked at the sign. Looked at Matt. Matt Jensen.

No way.

Seriously?

These two middle-aged hippies in clown makeup came running toward us, waving their arms. "Matty!" the woman shouted. "We missed you!"

She gave Matt a big hug and kiss. Bad idea — "Honey . . ." she said, recoiling. "You reek!"

Matt looked horrified. "Hi . . . Mom."

Sweet Lou leaned over toward us. "Those are Matt's parents?" he whispered. (Sweet Lou has always been a little slow.)

Matt introduced us to his parents, and then a teenage girl came running out and gave him a hug — must have been his younger sister. Who knew that Matt even *had* a family?

The sister wrinkled her nose. "Matt, you smell funky. Wait, wait. Let me guess what it is. I'm really good at this. Did you have blue cheese for lunch?"

"Nope." Matt grinned.

"No. Wait. I mean Gorgonzola? Feta?"

"No, I haven't eaten any cheese."

"Weird," the girl said, totally confused.

"I just cleaned out a row of Porta Potties," Matt said.

"Oh. Ah." She backed away. Fast.

Matt

The clowns were thrilled to have their baby back home. I was . . . less than thrilled. But I was also desperate.

"Could we borrow the bus?" I asked. "We've got to get to California. It's our last shot."

My dad laughed. "Oh, honey, guess what?" he said sarcastically. "Matt's back because he wants something."

She put her hand on his shoulder. "Honey, the important thing is Matt's here. And he brought his friends. That's a first."

You're right it's a first — and hopefully, it's a last. Probably I shouldn't tell them that, since I need to get the bus. Probably, I should just — oh, whatever.

"Look, I'm sorry, you guys," I said. "Truth is, you're still horribly embarrassing to me." I paused, hoping I hadn't crushed them. "But I came 'cause I didn't have anywhere else to go. And we need some help."

Dad totally pulled the parental trip on me. "Why haven't we heard from you? Why haven't you called?"

Well, the truth was working so far. . . .

"I guess I didn't understand why you left to join the circus," I said.

"And you need the bus?" he asked.

"To finish our mission." Now I was getting excited. "We're gonna prove something to ourselves even though no one respects us, no one listens to us . . . we're . . ."

"Outsiders?"

Dude. I hate it when my dad finishes my sentences like that. Especially when he's right. "I know we're not the parents you want us to be," he said, "but the truth is, we know what you're going through. We live it every day."

"You know, to most people," my mom added, "the clown life is a bit bizarre."

Ya think?

But then Dad came in for the kill. "Sort of like riding around on a skateboard all day."

Man, I know when I'm beat. "I'm sorry, you guys," I said. And this time, I meant it.

Dad came through in the end. "No, son. We're sorry. About trying to push you into clown college. About a lot of things."

"There's more to life than a pie in the face for you," Mom said. And then she said those words I'd been waiting years to hear. "And we accept that."

This whole conversation was totally blowing my mind. And I couldn't stop my mouth from workin' on its own. "I've been really mad at you for taking up this whole clown thing," I said. "But now I get it. You gotta do what makes you happy . . . I guess."

My dad patted me on the back. "Nothing in this life comes easy, Matt. But what's important is you're out there doing it."

Then he held out his hand. "You're a man now, son. We're proud of you."

Dude, a father-son handshake, just like in the movies. I reached out to grab his hand —

And a joy buzzer went off.

"Dad!" Okay, not *exactly* like the movies.

"Got ya!"

But, I guess, exactly like home.

Eric

I was surprised to discover that Matt's parents were clowns. Who wouldn't be? But that's nothing compared to the surprise I found waiting for me that night in the kitchen. I'd gone down to get something to eat, but when I saw Sweet Lou and Matt's sister, Denise, at the table with their heads bent together, I decided it might not be a good time. Of course, I couldn't help overhearing them a little. (Okay, okay, I was spying on them from the next room — but who could resist?)

"I can't believe you're Matt's sister," Sweet Lou said, shaking his head.

"Me either." Denise looked into Sweet Lou's eyes with that look of adoration I've seen so many times before. The weird thing was, Sweet Lou was actually looking back the same way.

"Same gene pool," he mused. "Are you sure you weren't adopted?"

"What's wrong with Matt?"

"Nothing," he said quickly. "Nothing at all. Except . . . I don't often find myself imagining what it would be like to kiss him."

Oh, boy.

That's when I left.

I couldn't wait to see the look on Matt's face when he found out that Sweet Lou and his little sister were . . .

Yuck.

Matt

The next morning, I was up early and ready to go. More than ready. Time to blow this joint and take the world by storm.

I met the guys out front — I thought they were going to fall over when they saw me.

"Whoa." Dustin took a step toward me. "Matt, you look . . . different."

What? A guy can't take a shower without the whole world noticing?

Even Sweet Lou looked impressed. "From slob to stud." He bit his lip and nodded in approval. "I see you've been taking some lessons from the master."

Finally noticed, did you?

I have to admit, I looked *good*. And clean. Which was, as Dustin said, different. But surprisingly, not in a bad way.

"Yeah, I thought I'd freshen up a bit," I said.

Eric patted me on the back — first time any of them have come near me voluntarily since we started this trip. "Welcome to the human race, my friend," he said. "I think you'll like it here."

Dude, that's taking things to the extreme, don't you think? I mean, I may have been nasty, but I wasn't an animal . . . was I?

Well, it was time to take off. I hugged my parents — in full clown gear — good-bye. "Thanks for letting us crash here. And thanks for the showers. We needed 'em. And the food, the laundry, the van, pretty much everything . . ."

"We're always here for you, son," Dad said.

Dude, my dad's pretty cool when he wants to be.

Of course . . .

I pulled a set of clown shoes out of the back of the bus and handed them back to my mother. "Don't think I'll be needing these," I told her.

She laughed. "Can't blame a mother for trying."

I guess not. "I'll see you guys," I said, waving good-bye. "Soon."

It would have been a great send-off, if I hadn't seen the look my little sister gave Sweet Lou before he hopped in the van.

Dude, I'm going to kill him!

Eric

I know I've said this before. A million times. But things were really turning around for us. We had a van, we had some food — Matt had even had a shower! (Though at the moment, he was popping a zit and splattering pus all over the rearview mirror, which just goes to show you that some things never change.)

We pulled into the lot at Oceanside, just in time for the pro skate event. This time, there was no way we could miss Jimmy Wilson — and no way, no way could he miss us.

As long as we could get through the dreaded registration area. Clearly, we'd need a better plan than we had last time. It was time for Plan C.

"Quick," I told Matt. "Find me a kid."

"I'm on it," he said, and took off, no questions asked.

What was taking so long? I stood around the registration table, waiting for Matt to show up with my kid. Finally, he showed up — but not with a kid. With a little person. You know, a grown-up guy who just happens to be really, really short. I started to say something, then thought better of it. You take what you can get.

At that moment, who should stroll by the posers. You know, the guys who tortured us back in Kansas. Great. Perfect timing. They smirked at me and sauntered past the registration area. Apparently, they were such studs they didn't even have to sign in.

Meanwhile, Matt had the guy by the neck. "Lemme go!" he was shouting. But Matt strong-armed him up to the registration table.

"Hi, I'm Eric Rivers," I told the clerk. "I'm here for little Timmy here." And I pointed to my "kid."

"My name's not Timmy —" he started, but Matt slapped his hand over the guy's mouth. Good for Matt.

"Timmy's from Create-a-Wish and he really wants to see us skate," I said, trying to sound pathetic. "It's like his last wish, and he really, *really* wants it to happen."

The registration clerk was unimpressed. "No skating unless you've been preregistered."

Had he even heard me? If at first you don't succeed . . .

I had Matt let the little person go. It was time to put all our cards on the table. It was time to beg. "Look, I'm not kidding you. Our team drove all day to get here. This is it for us." I decided to throw myself totally at his mercy — we had nothing left to lose. "It's our last chance before we go home and wonder what we might've been able to do. And I don't want anything from you but one chance to skate." I was practically shouting — I wanted to shake the guy. "Just let us skate!"

He just sounded bored. "Unless you're preregistered —" And then he looked up in surprise. "Which you are. I've got your name right here."

Huh?

"You do? I mean, of course you do," I babbled.

I was registered! I was skating in my first pro event! But why?

There was no time to figure it out — there was too much to see, too much to do. We stopped to watch a bunch of radical female skaters take on the street course. One of them looked familiar. . . .

"Whoa," said Matt, pointing. "Isn't that the chick you were chasin'? Dude, she's better than me!"

Oh, I am such an idiot.

When she finished her session, Jamie came over to us, sweating and grinning. I didn't say anything — I didn't even know where to begin.

Fortunately, she didn't hold my utter stupidity against me. "I put you and your friends on the list," she said. "Figured that if you could get out here for the event, you shouldn't be stopped by paperwork."

"I think I'm in love," I breathed.

"You don't have a problem with 'chick' skaters?" Jamie asked.

"Why should I?" I asked, puzzled.

"You shouldn't. But a lot of jerks on tour do," she answered.

"Hey, I'm completly embarrased. I was just so about my own trip, I didn't see you for who you are."

Jamie just looked at me. "Who am I to you?"

"I really can't wait to find out," I told her.

We just stood there for a minute, looking at each other. Then —

"Bring it," Jamie told me.

So I kissed her.

Dustin

I was proud of the kid. He'd gotten us this far, he hadn't let anything get him down, and now we were actually going to skate with the pros.

"I've been thinking," Eric said. "Whatever happens today, I'm glad we did this together."

"We've had a ride, all right," Sweet Lou agreed.

"Yeah," Matt said. "You got me outta your garage. For real. I'm talking to the clowns again. Oh, and the girls are starting to notice me . . ."

"That's 'cause you don't smell anymore." I paused for a second, thinking. "You know what, I'm bummed that I'm broke. But it's worth the money to be here. Even if we crash and burn."

We just stood there looking at each other for a second. Then Matt said, "I love you, Eric."

We all laughed, but I knew what he ment.

Matt pulled a clown nose out of his pocket and handed it to Sweet Lou. "Here My sister wanted you to have this. For good luck."

"Let's do this," Eric said.

It was time.

We headed for the ramp together. Over the loudspeaker, we could here the MC announcing our names: "Next up we've got Eric Rivers, Dustin Knight, Matt Jensen, and Sweet Lou Singer. Super Duper Skateboards!"

This was really it.

Eric

I stood at the head of the course with the guys, getting ready for the run. I thought I'd be nervous, but I wasn't. My team was with me, and there were a few other skaters on the pipe. The music was blasting and it sounded good. So I went for it. It just felt right. And I could see the guys skating all around me. We were the best we'd ever been.

We were awesome.

We were totally, unbelievably awesome.

Then I heard the MC again: "And finally, what you've all been waiting for, Jimmy Wilson, and the Dream Team!"

That was our cue to get off the course. So we did. But that was fine. We'd done our thing, and done it well. We grabbed our boards and headed off the course, past the full pipe. And who should be standing on top of it but my least favorite people — the posers. One of them was giving me a dirty look. But I wouldn't back down.

"No frontin'. You guys better turn in your skates," he sneered at me.

"Game of skate," I challenged him.

"You're on," he shot back.

I walked up the ramp, dropped my board, and the skate-off began.

He landed a trick. I matched it.

He landed another one. I did the same, only *better*.

It went on like that, with the two of us going trick for trick. Until . . . he tried doing my move. The 360 flip over the hip. He only went for a 180 . . . and he wiped out. Big time.

I stood at the top of the ramp. I could do it, I knew I could. And suddenly I realized everyone was watching. Not just my crew, not just his crew, but *everyone*. No one in the crowd was paying attention to Jimmy Wilson and the Dream Team anymore. They were watching me and the poser in our skate-off, and they were *waiting*. Waiting for me to finish it.

I took a deep breath, and I went for it. The 360.

It just felt right this time. And I landed it. Nailed it perfectly. I couldn't believe it. And the crowd . . . they went wild! Totally berserk. I saw Jamie's face in the crowd, and she was giving me the biggest, proudest grin ever.

The team ran up to me. But first they made room for the poser. It was quiet for a minute. Than I offered him my hand to shake.

The poser grinned and shook my hand up and down. "Yo dog, that was dope! You my boy, right here."

Then everyone else was back, crowding around me. Jamie was there, too.

"You were awesome, seriously," she said, throwing her arms around me.

"Best I've ever seen you skate," Matt cried.

"That counts for something," I said.

There was much celebrating and hugging. Even Matt's family showed up for the fun. Sweet Lou slung his arm around Denise.

"I think I'm in love," he said. "It's crazy — they're clowns."

Matt gave Sweet Lou a look, but then he must have decided to forget it.

"Thanks for coming," he said, giving his parents a hug. "I love you guys."

"Jimmy didn't see us," Dustin said quietly. He pointed, and we all turned just in time to see Jimmy's bus pulling put of the lot. "I'm sorry, man."

I took a deep breath. "Don't be. This isn't about Jimmy. It's about respect. I landed the trick." I looked at him, at Matt and Sweet Lou, and I knew why we were doing this. "It'll happen."

And you know what? I really believed it would.

After all, it was our destiny.

Dustin

So that was it. We turned around and went home.

No, really.

I couldn't believe it, either — I kept waiting for something else to happen. But nothing did. Could things have fallen into place so perfectly, just to end like this?

Apparently so.

So we were back to our old lives. Working dead-end jobs, hanging out, railin' through the streets. After a few weeks, it was almost like our trip had never happened. And don't get me wrong, it wasn't horrible.

But it wasn't great, either.

Eric, Matt, and I usually got together in the park after work; we all tried pretty hard not to mention what might have been.

"How's it goin' with the family business?" I asked. Eric's father had finally won — junior was working down at the hardware store. A dream come true for Rivers Senior. At least someone got what he wanted out of this whole deal.

"We're running a special on silicone sealant," Eric said, trying to sound enthusiastic. "Provides a tight weather-resistant seal."

I didn't even have the energy to think up an answer for that one.

Eric tried again. "Who's up for a quick session?"

Dude, I wish. But work called. "I can't," I said.

"You can."

"I can't. I got, like, three hundred ninety-two days to work before I can even start thinking about first semester again."

Eric didn't look thrilled about that, but he was cool about it. "All right. But remember — we're a team."

I grinned at him.

Maybe his optimism was starting to rub off on me.

Eric

I know you what you're thinking. You're thinking I must've been crushed. To just go back home and start working a regular old boring nine-to-five job. Like none of it had ever hapened. But it was okay. Really it was.

No one said anything, but I could see it in their eyes, every time they looked at me. Wondering how I was doing, if I was all right.

So okay, even I wondered that sometimes.

A lot.

But I still knew it was the right decision — and sometimes, you just have to trust that everything's going to work out in the end.

So that's what I was doing. Working in the hardware store, chilling with my friends, and waiting for everything to work out like I knew it would. Someday.

It sounded like Dustin was definitely out for the skating session. I turned to Matt, but he shook his head.

"I've got a date."

What?

"You do?" Dustin asked incredulously.

Matt looked a little embarrassed. "No . . . but I'm working on it." He pulled himself up a little straighter — Matt's like a whole different person these days, what with the clean clothes and the showering. I don't know what's gotten into him — but for once, it's not lice.

"I'm actually thinking about getting a job," he continued. "Maybe. I'm gonna need one if I'm gonna start dating."

Well, at least Matt got something — though who knows what — out of our little adventure. And hey, Dustin and I did, too, right?

"Dustin, look on the bright side," I told him. "We could've been slingin' chili all summer."

Dustin grinned. "True. Hey, you can't say that we didn't try. And *I* still can't believe Sweet Lou ran off to join the circus —"

"With my sister!" Matt added.

Yeah, it'd been a strange summer. I just couldn't believe it was over. "I know my body's here," I told them, "but in my mind, we're still out on the freeway somewhere."

I closed my eyes, thinking about the open road, open possibilities. I could almost feel the wind through my hair, almost hear the cheering crowd, the tour bus horns —

Hold on, that wasn't just in my head — I *did* hear a horn. And I knew that horn.

My eyes flew open, just in time to see a bus pull into the lot. Jimmy Wilson's bus! It was there right in front of us. For real.

"It's Jimmy's bus," I said stupidly. "What's Jimmy's bus doing here?" As if any of them would know the answer. We just stood there, frozen.

"What should we do?" Dustin asked.

No one knew, so we did nothing.

"Maybe he's lost . . . ?" Matt suggested halfheartedly.

Yeah, right. "And just happened to come here?" I asked.

"I feel weird just standing here," Dustin said. "Shouldn't we do something?"

But we didn't. We just stood there and watched the bus pull into a space. Turn off its engine. Open its doors.

And out he stepped. Jimmy Wilson. In the flesh.

I had no idea what to say to him. Apparently neither did Dustin or Matt. We just stood there, staring at him like a bunch of idiots.

Fortunately, he seemed to be used to stuff like that. So he just started talking. "Hey, I've been looking for you."

"Uh, hi," I managed. "Um, how did you find us?"

He gestured toward the bus with his thumb. "Oh, Jamie told me."

Sure enough, there was Jamie sitting by the windows. She was looking out at me with this enormous grin on her face. I grinned right back at her.

I suddenly realized Jimmy was talking to us while I was staring at Jamie like a lovesick jerk. " . . . and then I found your tour video on the bus . . ."

Matt and I slapped five — mission totally accomplished.

Jimmy kept going. "And then I heard about that insane skater who landed a three-sixty flip over the hip during my show . . ."

"Uh, sorry about that," I stammered.

"Don't worry about it," Jimmy said, laughing. "Anyway, we could use some fresh blood on the team, so we came to find you."

"All of us . . . on your team?" Matt was finally able to speak.

"Yeah, that's right."

I looked at the guys. None of us could believe it. All three of us. Pro skaters. It was our dream. Now we were a team, for real.

Jamie stuck her head out the window. "Hurry up before he changes his mind!" she called, winking at me.

The guys hopped on the bus, totally freaked and insanely happy.

"You just gotta believe," I murmured to myself.

I took one last look at the park, then hurried onto the bus to meet my destiny.

I plopped down next to Jamie and pulled her close.

There's always time for one last kiss.

Eric

One year later . . .

It was good to be home.

I'd headed right for the skate shop to grab some new gear — and sure enough, Greg was *still* working behind the counter. I laughed to myself, remembering the attitude he used to cop with me in the old days. Not anymore, dude.

"Hey, Greg, hook me up with one of my decks," I said.

He jumped to attention. "No prob, Eric." He turned to choose a board from his wall.

That's when I noticed the two skate punks watching me from the corner.

"That's Eric Rivers, man," one whispered to the other. "Here in person."

Greg tossed me the board, and I was about to head out when one of the kids got up his nerve to come up and talk to me.

"Hey, man. I saw your demo down in Springfield. You're awesome!"

I had to smile. He reminded me of someone — someone I used to know. Used to be.

"What's your name?" I asked.

"It's Mark."

I thought for a minute. Well, why not? "You want a new deck, Mark?" He looked like a little kid on Christmas morning. "Sure!"

I turned back to Greg. "Set these two guys up with my board," I said. "On me." I waved to the kids. "See ya, guys."

"Wait!" one of them called.

I stopped in the doorway.

"How can I get sponsored, man?" he asked.

Oh, kid. You wouldn't believe me if I told you. . . .

So, I went for the simple answer. Simple, but true: "Keep skating." It told the whole story.

All he had to do was believe.